Knot of Christmas Present

Knot of Christmas Present

KNOT A CHRISTMAS CAROL
BOOK TWO

IMOGEN KNOWED

Paperback ISBN: 979-8-9874825-5-1
Ebook ISNB: 978-1-972670-24-8

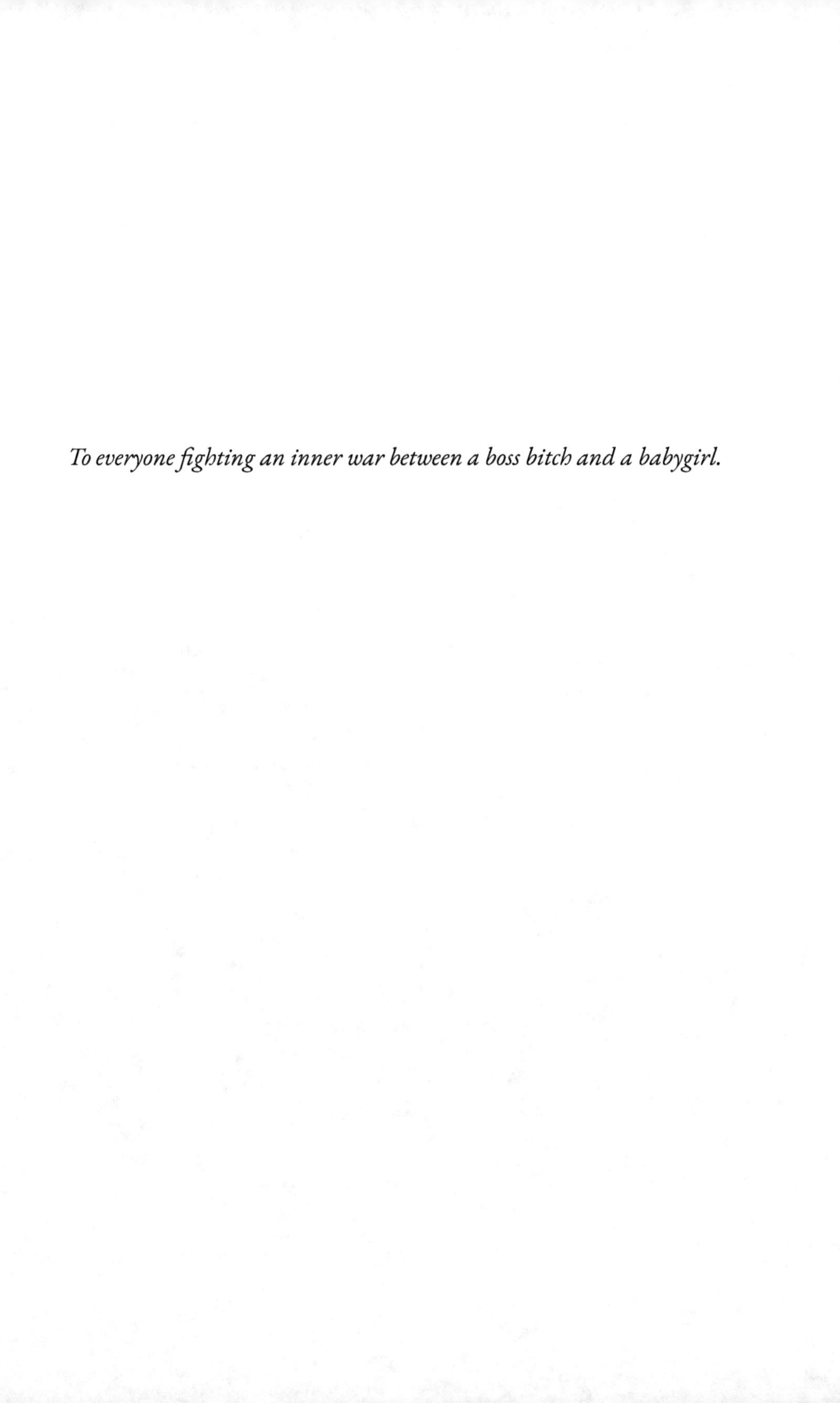

To everyone fighting an inner war between a boss bitch and a babygirl.

Content Warnings

This book has explicit descriptions of sexual acts.

While all sex is consensual, some acts may be considered dubious or coerced.

CHAPTER 1

I wake with her name in my mouth. I almost say it, almost out loud, but the only time I ever speak is in my dreams of her.

This time, it was as if she actually heard me. The first person to hear my voice in years, then she opened her mouth to my cock.

I...felt her.

She felt me.

The dim lights seep through the thin blanket covering my head as my surroundings come into consciousness. I'm in the business class section of a direct flight from Paris to Minneapolis. I'm lying on my side, my seat extended to a bed, and my back is to the aisle. I peer from under the blanket, craning my neck to see outside my cramped cubicle.

Fuck, I wish Air France offered La Première direct to Minneapolis.

All the windows are shuttered. The cabin lights are dim, and their soft glow makes my mind still feel hazy, like I'm still dreaming. I half suspect Evelyn to walk down the aisle toward me.

My heart is galloping as though I've been running toward her—or away from her—for miles. I readjust the blanket so that I'm once again hidden underneath it and press my palm against my erection, but the pain, the desire, remains.

The dream clings to me. She smelled like gingerbread. She was so beautiful. So real. I look at my trembling hand. I can almost...still feel her clenching around my fingers.

The dreams have always been vivid. They've always been so real. But this one. I could feel her. I could smell her. I could taste her. And she knew I was there. She could feel me. She saw me.

She could hear me.

Maybe it's because I'm finally on my way to meet her. My delusion is getting grander.

My phone, lying near my head, buzzes, then plays a song, alerting me that it's time to change my rut patch: 8:00 p.m. I blink at the screen and snooze the alert, returning my surgical mask to my face.

I raise the seat, transforming it from a bed to a chair, and lift the hood of my hoodie. The monitor in front of me displays flight information: local time is 1:01 p.m., with two hours until we land.

I need to change my patch. I can't rut out while I meet the literal woman of my dreams.

The air is too thick. My chest feels tight, as if the world has been vacuum-sealed around me. The cubicle beside me—one of five I purchased to create a buffer—is empty.

I lean into the aisle and peer down it to see if there is a clear path to the bathroom. A flight attendant stands near the bathroom door and locks eyes with me. She smiles. I snap back to my seat.

Please don't come over here. I don't need anything.

She approaches, and I shift uncomfortably in the seat and ensure the blanket covers my massive erection. She pauses in the aisle, and I pretend to be enamored with the instructional pamphlet in front of me: "...in the case of a rut or heat emergency, be sure to place the resulting oxygen mask over your own face first..."

The plane jerks slightly, and she braces her hand near my head, too close while saying, "Monsieur, would you—"

I raise my hand, shake my head, and offer a small nod that I hope conveys gratitude, not irritation. She smiles and moves on, not lingering too long.

Thank God.

I release some tension in my shoulders, close my eyes, and try to catch the remnants of the dream. Her voice. Her scent. The way her hair felt as I brushed my fingers through it. The way she opened her mouth to take my cock, as if she'd done it a million times. As if she knew me. Knew I was there.

Evelyn.

My phone buzzes again.

Fuck.

My eyes fly open, and I snooze the alert again.

I turn my head just a hint, looking for the flight attendant. I can't catch her eye and draw her attention to me again.

I don't see her.

I crane my neck, assessing the path to the bathroom again. It looks clear.

I place my backpack in my lap and retrieve the small plastic bag holding the day's rut patch and dose of pills. I put it in my hoodie pocket, grip my phone to my chest, and attempt to stand, but someone two rows in front of me enters the aisle and heads toward the bathroom first.

The alert buzzes again, and I snooze it.

I sit back and try to relax while I wait for the bathroom to become available. The plane hums, steady and relentless.

I just need to change my patch and take my meds. I'll feel better once I do that. My hand tightens around the bag in my pocket. My pulse beats in my throat. I focus on breathing. In through my nose. Out through my mouth. The mask warms with each exhale.

I wonder what she'll be wearing when I arrive. I hope it's that white silk blouse she had on earlier that opens slightly between the third and fourth button, providing a glimpse of the crest of her breasts whenever she laughs—or yells, which is more likely.

That's not real, Finn. That shirt doesn't exist.

It was just a dream.

In the dream, I left her tangled in a pile of flesh. I watched helplessly as three others pleasured her, but she couldn't hear me. She couldn't see me, while another buried his knot in her, bringing her the relief she so desperately needed.

That's how the dreams usually go. She goes about her day, and I just...exist there with her.

Every single time I sleep, I see her. My delusion has gotten so precise that it has convinced me I am seeing exactly what she's doing in that moment. I adjusted my sleep schedule so I could lie next to her in bed before she goes to work each morning.

But earlier, before the others pleasured her, I was the first. The first to help her with this difficult day. She saw me. She heard me. She smelled me.

It wasn't real Finn. You're obsession with her is just feeding your psychosis.

You'll meet her and see that it's all in your head. You'll see her office, you'll smell her, you'll hear her voice, and you'll realize it's not the same. The version of Evelyn you think you know...

Is.

Not.

Real.

My chest aches with wanting. Every thought of her burns somewhere deep within me.

I need her.

There are those who can't sleep. Well, I can't stay awake. Because every moment I am awake is a moment I am not with her.

Mine. She is mine.

It's been like this since I signed the contract to work with her almost a year ago. I thought I'd just be making music for the *Torchbearer* video game. I didn't realize I'd develop an obsession so deep that I've had to come up with some excuse to fly across the world and prove to myself once and for all she's not real.

Preston asked me to make the game's music. He said he already briefed the team on my specific working requirements. Apparently, the studio's CTO prefers to work under similar conditions, so they had no problem meeting my demands—already set up to support someone fully remote who preferred to communicate via text.

I like Preston. He doesn't push. I like the movie, too, so I agreed.

But the moment I saw Evelyn's digital signature on the contract, something shifted in me. It was as if the letters lifted off the page and pierced my heart, zinging right through me. From that moment, she has consumed my thoughts.

My therapist says it's psychosis brought on by my extended isolation. He says it's amplified from alpha hormones that have been repressed for too long, craving an omega. His first prescription was Risperidone. The second, after months of no improvement, was Clozapine. The third was "to go get laid."

He doesn't know I'm doing this. He'd probably advise against it. But none of his advice has worked so far, so I might as well try this.

I'll go to the studio. Meet her. See she's not who I dream about. I'll find an excuse not to work on the game her team is pitching to me today, then be done with this. Get my life back.

My phone buzzes, yet-a-fucking-gain. This time, the alert comes with a warning about the dangers of not taking my suppressants. It has a silly cartoon of an alpha rutting out.

Snooze.

Alpha. The moment my knot dropped, that fucking word has laced its way through every moment of my life. Tainting it with expectations I can't meet.

Power. Presence. Command. Words that don't describe me.

But when I'm on the stage, wearing the mask, playing my music for crowds of thousands. I can feel it: the alpha within me.

THNTS.exe. He's an alpha. Not me.

Even when I was Zain from Fate's Five, I didn't feel it. But the mask —it transforms me into the alpha I used to pretend to be.

When people see the skull mask, with its lights and animations, they assume it's a deliberate attempt at anonymity. Assume I'm a boisterous fuckboy underneath it all. Like I was...back then. Not that they know who I was...who I am.

They see the skull. They see the name. They hear the music. They think "power." They think "bringer of death." And, if they're cringe, they think "dropper of beats."

But I don't wear the mask for anonymity. Well, I do, but not for the reasons they think.

People think it's a bit. It's a gimmick.

But it's not.

I wear the mask because I can't look another person in the eye without it. It allows me to do what I love: play music. It allows me to exist within the world of others without their eyes upon me.

When I'm on stage, I wear the large animatronic mask, but the mask I wear now is just fabric. It only covers my mouth and provides just enough protection for me to walk among others, but not enough for me to truly interact with them.

Now, as I sit among empty cubicles, I feel like the most counterfeit alpha in existence. The world thinks we are meant to lead, to protect, to claim, to fuck, to procreate. But, as I look across the aisle, it doesn't feel like enough distance. I can still sense them: the other passengers, breathing, laughing, eating, existing.

Judging. Wanting. Expecting.

I haven't touched another person in twenty years.

I haven't spoken to another person in fifteen.

The last person who heard my voice said it sounded like death brought to life after so many years of silence. Now, the only living beings who hear my voice are my plants.

But every time I close my eyes, I speak to Evelyn.

And today she heard me.

She felt me.

No, Finn. No, it's in your head. You'll see.

She saw me. She did.

Another alert. This time, more insistent:

> Two dismissals remaining before alpha
> monitoring authorities are alerted.

Alpha. Ha, what a joke.

I tap out the alert and wait. My leg taps out an anxious beat. My fingers tap out an accompanying melody.

I guess I could just do it here.

The flight attendant returns, her omega perfume faint but sharp. She bends slightly, gesturing at the amenity table in front of me. "Something to drink?" Her eyes rake my body, and I can smell the arousal on her. I reach my hand to the back of my neck and ensure my gland covers are thoroughly in place. They are—thank God.

I need to take my meds, so I nod.

She hesitates, waiting for me to say something. But I don't. I won't.

"Water?" she asks. I smile, hoping she can see it in the crinkle of my eyes. I nod, hoping she'll be satisfied, leave the water, then leave.

She leans into my space, her cleavage nearly in my face. I back away, pressing myself as flat against my chair as I can.

Please. Please don't touch me.

She pulls the tray table out from the side table and places the glass upon it.

She doesn't move. Doesn't leave. Just stays in my bubble, her scent making its way through my mask and choking me. "Are you sure I can't do anything else for you, monsieur?"

I shake my head, perhaps too quickly, and close my eyes before she can meet them.

She must pull the blind up, because the light turns my lids red. She says, "The view is beautiful, isn't it?"

I shake my head and thread my hand upward, hoping I won't touch her, then yank the blind back down.

She makes a little startled noise that I'm sure she thinks is cute, but I find terrifying. Revolting. She mutters something that sounds like, "beautiful alphas, all the same," before leaving.

When her scent, her presence, no longer overwhelms me, I place my hand on my mask to ensure it's still firmly in place and finally reopen my eyes.

The mask is safety.

The mask is silence.

I press my palm against my sternum. My heart is wild, ready to explode in my chest.

Omegas always do that: get in my space. Even the ones with alphas. This one, at least, doesn't seem to recognize me from my supposed glory days. Probably too young. Even though the internet has immortalized me as the front man for one of the most successful boy bands of all time, my face is no longer at the forefront of everyone's mind.

I used to love it. I used to take from them whatever they wanted to give. My band—my pack—and I were unstoppable. Climbing the charts and claiming hearts. Running trains through omegas after every show.

But that was then. When I didn't hide my face. Didn't hide my voice. Before the expectations became too much to handle.

When I had a pack...

I take my anti-psychotics, my hand trembling as I turn my face to the window, raise my mask, and bring the pills and water to my mouth.

I swallow, hoping they'll bring some relief. They never do.

Someone exits the bathroom, and I wait a moment before finally deeming the path clear.

I unbuckle my seatbelt and stand, stretching, but not lingering too long. My muscles tremble from stagnation. When I move, I can feel the faint brush of my scent lifting. It makes me self-conscious, but airplanes are pretty good at filtering scents, since on-flight ruttings can cost them millions of dollars in legal fees. So there's likely no one close enough to notice.

I move with a speed that I hope doesn't bring too much attention, dipping my head and closing my eyes to avoid all theirs.

I'm fine.

I've been telling myself that since I handed the keys to my flat over to the plant sitter. I said it to myself when I went through customs at Roissy. I said it to myself when I waited in the lounge and emailed Evelyn my itinerary. I said it to myself when I boarded the plane. And I said it when I sat in my seat and looked at my reflection in the window seven hours ago as the plane began its ascent.

You're fine.

You're doing this.

I am not fine.

CHAPTER 2
Preston

I'm mostly naked, wearing nothing but a pair of boxer briefs and socks. I stand in the middle of the suite, arms stretched out like I'm one of those character models Evelyn showed me when we first started working together. The outfit I last tried on was not quite right. None of them have been.

The idea of her has been in my head for a year. And now I'm supposed to meet her.

In two hours.

Maybe less.

I'm not sure what time it is, and look at my wrist, which doesn't have a watch. Ben notices. As my chief of logistics, aka assistant, it's his job to notice, but he noticed these things even before I put him on my payroll. "We're fine on time," he says. "Two hours until you have to leave."

Talia moves past me, a blur of black clothing, facial piercings, and precision, clutching two green shirts. "Choose," she instructs. I reach for one, then change my mind midair. My hand hovers uselessly.

Felix, who's been silently orchestrating some miracle with my hair, catches my hesitation in the mirror. "He's spiraling," he says casually.

"I'm not spiraling," I say, too fast.

He meets my eyes in the reflection. "Sure you're not." He returns to his work, comb in hand, and gives Derek a glance that says, "Help me out here."

Derek, my "energy and endocrinology alignment coach" (which is one of those job titles you make up so you can pay your packmates to hang out with you), holds up a crystal the size of a pear around my scent glands.

"You're giving off a really bad vibe...and scent," he says gravely. "Your hot chocolate is all...grey...so is your aura." He scrunches his nose at me, then bends to double-check my rut suppressant patch is firmly in place.

I scoff. "I think it's called a panic attack, Derek."

"Why is he freaking out so much about this?" Talia asks Felix, folding the green shirts over her arm. "Isn't it just some date?"

Felix clicks his tongue and says, "Not just some date. He's meeting that omega who runs the studio making the *Torchbearer* game."

Talia's eyes go wide. "Why didn't you jackasses tell me!? Of course you can't wear fucking green!" She runs out of the room to fetch yet another shirt, muttering something about "undertones."

Ben rolls his eyes and says with a level of annoyance he reserves for Talia, "I did tell you, Tali! You've just been rut-rambling and weren't listening."

This morning, I hung up my meeting with Evelyn, and after approximately thirty minutes of melting down, tossing my cufflinks across the room, rummaging through my clothes, and trying to do my own hair, Ben and Derek stormed in.

Ben paced around the room, tapping away at his tablet, chastising me for not calling them in. "I had to hear it from Bob? Not my best fucking friend." Once he got the message, he yanked Derek out of bed and summoned the rest of the pack with a group text reading:

SOS HAIR MAKEUP WARDROBE

Derek, like usual, wasn't much help for the first fifteen minutes. While I tried to explain to Ben that I didn't want to assemble the pack on a holiday, Derek paced around the room, cursing its bad feng shui.

Derek feigned a faint, then, after I pulled him from the ground, rushed around the room, rearranging the furniture.

By the time Derek finished pushing the massive bed to the other side of the room, Felix strolled in, pushing the massive cases of hair and makeup products he takes everywhere with him, just in case I have a beauty emergency.

Talia arrived only about five minutes ago. She walked in with half my winter wardrobe and stars in her eyes. She's been gushing about the "cutest little, bonded, omega and beta twinks" she hooked up with last night, and rambling about how we should all move to Minneapolis.

The five of us have been a platonic pack since we starred on a sitcom together as kids. We don't fuck, well, Derek and Ben fuck, and yeah, we all have fucked a few times, but we're not that kind of pack. We're the trauma-bonded kind of pack, not the mate-bonded kind of pack. I'll just say, child labor laws weren't that great back then, still aren't for child actors, but we made it out alive, and mostly unscathed. I'm the only one who continued acting after that, though.

Talia rushes in, holding multiple burgundy shirts. "This is your color." And she's right. It is.

I stand still while Talia unbuttons me, replaces the shirt, and buttons me again.

I'm fidgeting, feeling restless in my skin, and pulling at the shirt.

Derek waves the crystal over my head, whispering, "Manifest calm."

Talia steps back, assessing me like a painting she's not sure she likes, and harumphs. Derek waves the crystal over her head, and she swats him away, kicking at his shins, before returning her critical eyes to me, watching my reflection, and likely assessing how the fabric moves with my body.

After a few more tries, eventually Talia resolves the shirt situation, picking black, not burgundy. She stands back, smug in her decision.

Felix tucks those little napkins in my shirt to protect it from the magic he's about to perform on my face. "We going full face?" he asks.

"I don't think it's a good idea."

"Planning on getting really close and really sweaty?"

"Well...I mean...if things go as planned, yeah."

"Alright, we'll go for light concealer then. Luckily, your skin looks pretty good today," Felix says, scrutinizing my skin. "This couldn't have come at a better time in your rut cycle. Plus, those new suppressants are wonders for your skin."

"Yeah, thank God," I say, because I can't imagine how nervous I'd be right now if I were also breaking out. Derek beams, waiting for praise, like the beta he is, so I say, "'Thank, Derek,' I mean. He convinced me to switch brands." And, I'm happy I did. Not just because of the skin, but because this fucking patch is so strong I'm honestly surprised I can get it up at all. And...I'm pretty sure Evelyn is in heat.

I look past my pack and smile when I catch sight of a specific corner of the hotel room. When I was on my call with Evelyn, she was off her game. Frazzled. I could tell something was going on with her, but I wasn't sure what it was. But then, she accidentally showed me her phone screen, and that's when I knew she was in heat. I only saw it for a second, but she was watching an alpha, knotting into an omega, with this exact room as the backdrop.

In that moment, I knew three things: one, I was right, this hotel room was used for filming pornos; two, she was in heat; and three, I had to go to her. Actually, four things. The fourth being I needed to wash my hands and not eat anything off the table in that back corner.

And that's why I'm more anxious than I normally would be. I'm anxious to meet her, sure, but I'm feeling a bit like a sleazebag. I'm trying to convince myself that the high-powered suppressants running through me make this all okay, but I'm not really sure I have convinced myself.

My phone buzzes. Another text from Mom. I stare at the message.

MOM

All I want is for you to be happy, darling.

Felix whispers, brushing a fluffy wand over my cheeks, "You gonna tell your mom?"

"Absolutely not." Then I reconsider. "Well, maybe." Then, I reconsider, again shaking my head, "I don't want to get her hopes up. You know how she is."

"Oh yeah," he laughs.

Felix has also heard the lectures from my mom: "Why won't you five just form a bonded pack, already? Two betas and three alphas. All you'd need is an omega. Between you, Felix, and Talia, it should be easy for you to find an omega."

I've tried to explain to her that it's not like we haven't considered it. It's not like we hadn't tried. Our scents, while working together in a comforting blend, just don't..."vibe like that," as Derek would say. But, really, the main problem is our sexual compatibility just isn't there. Felix is asexual/aromantic and doesn't want anything to do with omegas or "fluids of any kind." Talia is only interested in small, male omegas and finds the four of us to be "kinda big and gross." Ben and Derek are content with just each other and "not looking to get knotted." And then there's me: the hopeless romantic who's been so afraid of committing to the wrong person, I barely go on a first date, let alone a second.

My pulse is climbing. I've done a hundred red carpets, a thousand interviews, and smiled through the blur of it all. That's easy. But this isn't that. This is one woman. The woman. The woman for me. I've only ever seen her through screens. And the way my heart flutters just at the thought of being in the same city as her, you'd think I was the one meeting a movie star.

It's not a parasocial relationship. It's not. We are actual friends. Right?

Talia doesn't spend nearly as much time deliberating trousers before she has me step into a pair. The belt and jacket are a whole other matter, though.

"Pick the watch, then I'll pick the rest of your accessories," she says, presenting two watches to me. I pick the least ostentatious one.

I think about the first time I saw Evelyn. I knew then. I knew she was the one. The omega I needed. And now here we are. Or almost. I look at the watch as I put it on. Less than an hour.

"Where are your new cufflinks?" she asks.

"Um...I'm not sure," I say, not wanting to admit that I ripped them out in a fit of rage and threw them across the room earlier.

Talia hands me a different pair of cufflinks. They're tiny, gold, impersonal. My fingers don't quite cooperate as I try to put them in, and I can feel the heat creeping up my neck. It's ridiculous, but it feels like failure. Like, if I can't manage this, what business do I have walking into a room to meet her?

Talia quietly takes over, fastening them for me without comment. She's known me long enough to know when to say nothing.

When she finishes, I take another look at the clock: fifty minutes.

Ben must notice me checking the watch because he says, "We're fine on time," and I nod, not quite believing it.

Felix hums behind me, some unrecognizable tune, maybe just to fill the silence.

Maybe to calm me.

Probably that.

I tap my foot, the energy in my body needing somewhere to go.

I wonder what Evelyn's doing right now. I wonder what the office looks like. I wonder if she'll even like me.

Felix steps back, satisfied. "Hair's done. Don't touch it."

"Wouldn't dream of it," I say, running my hand through my hair.

He squints. "You already did."

"I didn't."

"You just did."

He pats my shoulder and starts packing up his brushes.

I give myself a final check in the mirror. The reflection doesn't match the inside. On the outside: calm, composed, effortless. Inside: chaos.

I break away from them, now free from the confines of Felix's hair and makeup styling.

I pace. I can't stop moving now. My body wants motion. My mind wants stillness.

I can't tell if it's getting hotter in here or if it's just me. I pull the little paper things from my shirt. They're suffocating me.

I pace. Every step feels too loud. My hands can't stay still; they keep finding my pockets, my watch, the cufflinks.

What if she thinks I'm obnoxious? What if she thinks my scent is too sweet for an alpha—she wouldn't be the first omega who said that to me.

Derek steps in front of me and says, "Preston, you're doing that thing."

"What thing?"

He grabs my shoulders and says calmly, "That thing you do when you're trying to jump to the future." He lets out a deep breath, and I mimic him. "Stay here for a second. In this moment. In the present. It's the only moment that's real."

I nod, but my brain's already gone ahead—to the elevator, to the lobby, to the moment I see her. I can't stop it. My mind keeps building it like I'm rushing toward my doom or my happily ever after.

Talia joins us, smooths the fabric on my shoulder, then rests her hand near Derek's. Ben and Felix join them, placing their hands on me, grounding me.

Derek says, "Breathe," and we all do, in unison, as a pack.

CHAPTER 3
Evelyn

This guy is already getting on my nerves.

I'm trying very hard to at least appear like a woman in control of her shit, rather than a frazzled mess who's hiding behind a large cup of coffee and her desk.

The coffee isn't helping. Neither is the seven-foot-tall alpha sitting in the chair in front of me, who's been following me like a lost puppy who finally found his way home. Chris is scrolling through his phone, lounging in the chair across my desk like it was made for him, even though he's so big he barely fits in it.

He still looks like a total mess. Bare forearms. Shirt misbuttoned. Tie gone. Hot as fuck. Sperm and slick all over him. That annoying, effortless confidence even the supposed humble alphas have.

Breathe, Evie.

You are the boss here. Not his boss, but this is your domain. Alphas inherently respect territory, and this is your territory.

I can absolutely handle one overgrown man with good shoulders and a devastating smile...and the biggest dick I've ever seen.

I won't think about that.

"Chris," I say, taking a deep breath, "you really don't have to watch me work."

He looks up slowly, a smile tugging at one corner of his mouth. "But I want to. You're cute, and I like looking at you." I roll my eyes so hard I feel like I can see the inside of my skull, and unfortunately, I also blush because, as much as I hate it, I like being called cute...sometimes.

He leans forward. "You're flushing," he observes. "You sure you're okay to work?"

I resist the urge to throw my stapler at him. "I'm fine."

"Is your heat flaring?"

"I'm fine."

"Are you sure, because you smell—"

"Finish that sentence, and I will throw my stapler at your head."

He laughs, a deep, low sound that makes my pussy scream, "Wouldn't it feel good if you sat on his face while he did that?" My brain, however, reminds me he's a client. A potential one, anyway, and the deal with him still hasn't been signed. I have to play nice...well, nice-ish.

The problem is, it's hard to look at him and think *client*. The whole "I've been looking for you for twenty years, and we're a scent-matched pack" thing caught me off guard, lowered my defenses, and spoke to a part of me I try to keep locked up. But, after he locked into me, I'm now able to keep my legs locked tight, and that part of my heart is locking back up, too.

Thank God. I really don't have time for this shit.

He continues with that overbearing alpha-bullshit that assumes he knows better than me and says, "You're going to burn yourself out trying to work through this heat. You should let me—"

"I don't need—"

"Help?" he finishes.

"Yes. Exactly. I don't need help."

He studies me for a long moment. Then, softer: "I think you do."

"Chris, this is not your problem."

"Feels like it is."

"Well, it isn't."

"You could just talk to me, you know. You don't have to pretend to work to avoid talking to me. Or you could rest. I'm not going to judge you."

"And what's that supposed to mean?"

"That you're working yourself into the ground because it's easier than admitting you like having me here."

"Wow. That sure is presumptuous of you. I see that alpha ego is as big as the rest of you."

He smirks. "You were thinking it."

"I was thinking about quarterly earnings."

"Sure you were."

I harumph. "You're insufferable."

"And you're adorable when you're mad."

My face turns bright red from flattery and fucking rage. "Stop calling me adorable. I'm the CEO of a multibillion-dollar corporation."

"Exactly," he says, like that proves his point somehow.

"Chris, you really should go and let me get to work."

"I will."

"When?"

"When I'm sure you've eaten."

"Tim will be back with food any minute."

He smiles. "Then I'll wait."

"You're going to drive me insane."

"Probably," he says. "But at least you won't be alone."

He goes back to looking at his phone as if his presence isn't so supremely looming that I could actually get anything done with him around.

He knows how much fucking space he takes up, right?

I give up and try to concentrate on my work. There's no winning an argument with someone who thinks every retort is flirting. I take a deep breath and try to ignore him.

I open the internal messaging app to ping Styles:

Evelyn Charles

> So, update on the Torchbearer presentation:
> I fumbled it.

Elizabeth Styles

Let me guess:
you opened the game before turning on the controller.

Evelyn Charles

Yes

Elizabeth Styles

Yeah, figured that would happen.
You looked like shit.
Did you go home yet?

Evelyn Charles

No.
He's coming into the office to see the build.

Elizabeth Styles

You can't be serious.
Evelyn, you're obviously in heat.

Evelyn Charles

PRE HEAT!!

Elizabeth Styles

I don't know who you think you're lying to, me or you.

Evelyn Charles

It's fine.
I've taken care of it.

Elizabeth Styles

And what exactly does that mean?

I almost giggle like a schoolgirl, but stop myself. I purse my lips and glance at Chris, who's now watching me like I'm his favorite form of entertainment. "Seriously," I tell him. "Don't you have something better to do? Or an ego to polish? You can't just camp out here."

"Can't?" He raises an eyebrow.

I glare.

He shrugs and leans back, stretching his long legs out in front of him. "I'm fine here. You don't look fine, though. You are looking really pale. You need to eat."

There it is again—that protective, hovering instinct that's supposed to be flattering but mostly feels like static in my brain. "Is that your medical opinion, doctor?"

"Actually, yes, it is. I won't feel comfortable leaving you alone until you've eaten."

I groan. *This fucking guy.*

I pull out my phone. "Tim is on his way with the food."

"Like I said, I'll wait."

I raise my voice. "Chris. Listen to the words that are coming out of my mouth. I. Am. Fine. I am a big girl who has fed herself every day of her adult life without your help. I can continue to do so."

"But you're in he—"

"PRE-HEAT!"

"Either way, as your alpha, I can't just leave you alone until I know you'll be okay."

My alpha?! The audacity of this dude to presume he is my alpha.

I want to fucking scream.

Where the fuck is Tim with the food? I'm hungry and am mad that admitting that somehow feels like Chris is right and I should eat something. I grit my teeth and say, "I'll ask Tim where he is with the food."

EVELYN

eta on the food?

TIM

in my hands. 10 mins max

Please hurry. He's smothering me.

I glance at the clock on my monitor. Thirty minutes until my meeting with Preston Geist. Preston is an actor—a fucking hot one. An alpha. And our biggest client. Which means I need to walk into that meeting exuding composure and capability, not...whatever this mess is.

He's coming to the office so I can show him the latest build of his game. But I was also kind of hoping I could use this opportunity to sit on his pretty face. Which is something I would have wanted even if I weren't in heat. Pre-heat!

Maybe Bobby can save me from Chris's smothering. Where is he?

eta on the clothes, Bobby?

BOBBY ANDREWS

Here now. On my way up.

Thanks, Bobby.

FYI, I located the paperwork we need to fill out to declare that we are a pack with HR. Would you like me to forward it to you and Tim?

I squeeze the bridge of my nose.

God damn it. I cannot deal with this shit right now.

I choose not to respond.

I let out a deep, frustrated sigh when Chris chimes in, "You'll feel better after you eat."

I snap back, "I'll feel better when you leave."

"Same difference," he says with the smuggest smirk.

I am going to murder this mother fucker.

He's a client, Evie. You can't fuck AND murder your clients.

Then a message from Tim pops in:

TIM RIVERA

hey, so, we should probably talk about what happened. right?

Note to self: don't sleep with any more of your employees. And definitely stop scent-matching with clients. HR is going to implode.

I choose not to respond to that message, too.

I don't really know what to say to them right now.

My computer pings incessantly as Styles messages me, and my rage and frustration boil. I feel so out of control.

I can't control my body.

I can't control this fucking guy. And now, I don't think I can even control my own employees.

I should probably talk to Tim and Bobby about this pack thing. Scent-matching is a load of hogwash. I was just caught up in the moment. I don't have time for the whole talking about my feelings nonsense, though. But Bobby and Tim are important to me, and I need to be considerate of their feelings.

But this guy...

I look at Chris, who's once again watching me. I really don't want to bring another alpha into my life. They always try to boss me around.

"Hey," Chris says, as if he wants to prove my point. "You're spiraling, aren't you?"

"No! I'm *working*," I correct him.

"Well, whatever you're working on is causing your stress to spike. Your scent is shifting."

I pinch the bridge of my nose. "I don't need you monitoring my stress levels. Or my scent."

He grins that stupid, cute, confident alpha smile. "Then stop smelling so sweet."

I repress a grin and maintain my resting bitch face. He keeps fucking flirting with me. He keeps making me want to like him, and I fucking hate it. "Well, maybe if I didn't have a fucking seven-foot alpha breathing down my god damn neck, I wouldn't feel stressed!? Did you think of that!?"

He looks...hurt. Actually hurt. I turn my chair away from him, unable to look at him, and angry that I actually feel kind of bad. But these god damn reflective walls show those adorable puppy dog eyes.

Note to self: get real walls.

He clears his throat, and his reflection shows that he has the decency to actually look a little ashamed. "I'm sorry, Evelyn, I'm just worried about you."

I spin my chair toward him, anger overtaking me. *I will not feel sorry for him. I will not let him feel sorry for me.* "Why do you care so much?"

"Because your welfare has consumed my thoughts for almost twenty years."

"And I have done just fine without you in my life, as you can see," I spit.

"I do see. You're quite impressive."

"For an omega you mean?"

"No. I don't. You're quite impressive. Period. End of sentence."

I squint at him. *What's his game? There's no way he doesn't have some misogynistic or omegaphobic agenda.*

He's grinning at me, and I can't tell if he's patronizing me or not. His eyes, which I had thought were brown, look green now that all the lights are on.

Just like a Christmas tree.

I scowl. "Why do you keep looking at me like that?"

"Like what?"

"Like that," I say, pointing at his face and attempting to emulate the big-eyed look he's giving me.

He rubs the back of his head. "I'm still feeling a bit of the rush... from knotting someone for the first time."

My heart stops.

"That...that was your first time?"

"Yeah, no one's ever been able to take it before. But you..." He leans forward and puts his elbows on my desk, propping his chin upon his hands. "You took me so well. It's like you were built for me."

I sputter. Heat rushing to my loins.

Fuck. Don't get all sappy and horny, Evie.

I break eye contact with him.

He nearly whispers, dropping his voice to a seductive tone, "Hey... did you like it? Did you like my cock?"

I squeeze my legs together and try to stop the perfume of gingerbread that puffs out of me, but I can't. It's met with a spray of pine, snow, and safety. It lowers my defenses and makes me want to cuddle with him.

But I won't admit it. I won't. Instead, I say, "It was...sufficient. Yes."

He leans back and folds his arms. "Sufficient? Wow, I was worried I wouldn't do a good job, but shit. I haven't gotten sufficient on a report card since freshman microbiology."

He looks actually disappointed in himself, and I hate that this guy is making me feel bad for him, but I add, "It was...more than sufficient. It was good. I appreciate your assistance."

His eyes narrow a fraction. "So you admit it meant something."

Oh, for the love of fucking God, this guy. "It meant I was in a physiological state that required assistance. Medical. You should understand that as a doctor. It's biology, not destiny."

"Could be both."

"Or you could be delusional."

He grins. "You always this romantic?"

I glare, but my pulse betrays me.

The truth is, I *like* him. That's the problem. He's infuriating, confident, and kind in a way that sneaks up on you. And the way he looks at me—it's like he already decided something I haven't agreed to: that I'm his mate.

I snap, "I have work to do!" and turn back to my computer monitor that has been pinging incessantly. I am greeted by an increasingly urgent wall of text from Styles peppered with various gifs and emojis.

When it comes to verbal communication, Styles is curt, stoic, mature, and to the point. But when it comes to chat messages, she shows the silly, girly side of her.

I sneak a glance at Chris to ensure he can't see my screen before responding.

Evelyn Charles

So I let the alpha client Tim brought in knot me. It's no big deal. But, I'm feeling better now and should be able to make it through the day.

Elizabeth Styles

orly!?
What's he look like?

I sneak another glance at him, repress another smile, then respond.

Evelyn Charles

Annoyingly handsome. Huge: at least seven feet. You know the pro gamer Chris Yore? It's him.

Elizabeth Styles

No fucking shit!?
He's a doctor now, right?

Evelyn Charles

Yeah

Elizabeth Styles

Noice

My feet swing giddily under the desk. I stop them and plant them firmly on the ground.

Evelyn Charles

Get this: he's the alpha that saved me during my first heat.

Elizabeth Styles

OMFG

Evelyn Charles

AAAAAAND!!! He says Bobby, Tim, and I are his scent-matched pack.
Which is total and utter bullshit, obviously.

Elizabeth Styles

Gah, alphas are always trying to pull that "we're scent-matched, we're meant to be"
But bringing Bobby and Tim in. That's a new one.

Evelyn Charles

ikr!?

Elizabeth Styles

Wait...does that mean you, Bobby, Tim, and the alpha... ????

Evelyn Charles

Yeah

Elizabeth Styles

Woooooooah
What are you gonna do?

Evelyn Charles

I gotta get rid of him.

Elizabeth Styles

But what about Bobby and Tim?

Evelyn Charles

I don't know. They really seem bought into this whole "we're a pack thing."

Elizabeth Styles

Well, keep me updated.
You good to present Torchbearer live to PG?

Evelyn Charles

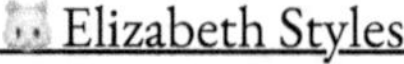

Elizabeth Styles

Good luck, E. You'll need it

CHAPTER 4
Preston

I check my watch again: thirty minutes.

Talia's voice cuts through the air. "Shoes." She says, holding them up. She kneels, placing them on my feet, and when she starts futzing with the laces, I feel an irrational need to stop her, to do something for myself. "I've got it," I say, crouching. My fingers feel clumsy on the laces.

Talia, still kneeling in front of me, doesn't move. "You okay?"

"Yeah. Great."

It's a lie. My heart's beating in my throat, and my brain feels full of static.

She stands and ushers me to a chair. I sit on the edge, trying to breathe, but every inhale feels like it has to fight its way in. It's the same chair I sat in when I last video called with Evelyn.

I think about how this must look—this absurd little performance of transformation. Four people are working on me, and I still feel like I'm falling apart. Talia ties my shoes, then stands, putting a reassuring hand on my shoulder.

I want to tell them to go. I want to be alone. But the idea of being alone with my thoughts feels worse.

Derek appears at my side and says, "You'll want to eat something before you go."

"I can't."

"You should."

"I really can't."

He doesn't argue further. He just presses an alpha power bar into my hand. "Eat it in the car, then."

Ben hands me a small bottle of water. "Drink."

I do—half of it. The taste is metallic, or maybe that's just my nerves.

I'm frozen, I can't move.

I stare at the floor, my mind wandering—racing. The others busy themselves and let me sit with my thoughts for a moment. Talia gathers the discarded clothes and folds them into garment bags. Felix packs up his kit and wipes off his brushes. Derek continues to fiddle with the furniture's arrangement while Ben taps away at his tablet, orchestrating something.

I catch my reflection in one of the millions of reflective surfaces, and something in me wants to apologize to it—for being uncertain, for not being better at this, for needing them to help me with so much.

And suddenly, I'm no longer "good on time," I'm running out of it. Ben steps in front of me, forcing me to forfeit my staring contest with the floor. "Ten minutes."

The words hit like a countdown. Ten minutes until everything I've imagined either becomes something or disappears.

"Right," I say. Time now stands still. But I don't. I remain seated. Everything comes to a hum in my brain.

It's absurd, I think. All of this. The team of people whose job it is to make me look like myself. *What does it matter what I look like if my voice shakes when I say her name? How will I be able to do this without them?*

They all stop their hurried movements at the same time. Felix stops packing up and leans on the table near me, folding his hands at his lap. Talia sits on the edge of the chair next to me. Ben hovers between me and the door.

Derek kneels in front of me. "Try to breathe," Derek says. "In through the nose, out through the mouth."

I obey, because it's easier than thinking. The first few breaths are shallow, but then something starts to shift. My shoulders drop a fraction.

"Better?" he asks.

"Almost."

Felix reassures me, "Just play the part, Preston. You can do this."

"It's been so long since I've acted."

Talia adds, "They say it's like riding a bike."

I don't respond. Just staring past them.

"She'll like you," Ben says simply. "People do."

I smile, but the feeling in my chest is hollow. "Until they don't anymore."

Felix nods once, reading something in my face. "Just be...human," he says. "The things you try to hide: that's what she'll like about you. I promise."

And somehow that's exactly what I needed to hear. I nod, resolve finally setting in, and stand.

This sets off a flurry of movement amongst them. The calm that they all coalesced on to soothe me shifts to the methodical hurry of a team of people trying to get one overgrown manbaby out the door.

Talia says, "Pres, jacket, please."

I turn. She's holding it up. The color—burgundy—looks perfect. Of course it does. She always gets it right. I shrug it on and appreciate its weight, its structure.

Felix reappears, inspecting me from a few feet away. "Don't slouch."

I straighten, automatically.

"It's cold as balls outside," Talia says. "You'll need a coat." She opens the closet and chooses one for me.

I shake my head. "No. I'll sweat. I can handle the cold. I won't be outside long."

She doesn't argue. Just puts the coat back in the closet, then steps closer and fixes a stray thread on my sleeve. She crouches in front of me, checking the hem of my trousers. "Don't fidget," she says, voice softer now. "You'll wrinkle the jacket."

"Sorry."

She looks up at me, giving me that look they all give me when they know I'm teetering on the edge. "You'll be fine," she says. "You always are."

I look at the door, waiting for Talia to finish, and I imagine the moment when I'll see Evelyn, in person, for the first time. Her eyes will meet mine, then she'll either maintain eye contact or look away. That's when I'll know. That's when she'll know. I have one moment. That one. If I don't nail it, it doesn't matter what else I do; it'll never materialize if that moment isn't perfect.

I can feel the sweat on my palms. I wipe them on my trousers, then instantly regret it.

Talia raises an eyebrow. "Don't ruin my work."

"Sorry."

"Stop saying sorry," she says, standing and patting me on the shoulder.

I open my mouth to argue, then close it.

Her hand grips my shoulder now. "Seriously, Pres. You'll be fine." She smiles and looks at me with that quiet mixture of fondness and exasperation only people who know you well and still like you can have.

Ben gets a phone call. "Yeah. Okay. Thanks. He'll be down in a minute." When he hangs up, he approaches me and says, "Car's ready whenever you are."

The air feels charged now. Everyone's just waiting for me to move—as if my movement will discharge the air somehow.

I move toward the door. My pulse is still too fast, but at least it's steady now.

Talia catches my sleeve as I hover by the door. "You'll be fine," she says again, quieter this time.

I nod. "I know."

And for a moment, I almost believe it.

They hang back, standing together, watching me as my hand hovers by the knob. It's strange how quickly they start to fade once I'm facing away from them. All the voices that kept me upright for the past few hours, past few decades, turn into a kind of distant hum.

It's like...I'm leaving them...

I can't leave them.

They must see the panic returning to my eyes again, because they rush to me to make one final fuss. Like a flock of mother hens taking care of a sole baby chick. Talia adjusts the lapel of my jacket, fingers quick and deliberate. Felix smooths an invisible strand of hair into place. Each of them adds some tiny finishing touch as if the right combination of gestures will hold me together once I'm outside.

When they're done, they all take a step back, and I am overwhelmed by how much I love them all. How much I need them.

I have to do this alone.

I can't do this alone.

They're my pack.

I can't leave them.

My hands hang awkwardly at my sides. I take a slow breath and hold it, then let it out.

Ben clears his throat gently. "You should go."

I nod, but I don't move. My mind flicks through every version of what might happen next. It feels like walking through this door is the end—the end of my current pack and the start of a new one.

I think about telling them how much I appreciate this—their calm, their precision, their patience—but the words feel clumsy in my mouth. So I just look at them, hoping they understand.

I think about changing my mind and staying with them.

Talia reads it on my face. "We all want this for you," she says softly, "it's going to happen. It'll be great."

"Go get your omega," Derek says, grabbing Ben's hand.

"Start your pack," Felix says.

"We'll still be here," Ben smiles.

Derek jokes, "Yeah, who else will pay me to wave crystals around them?"

We all laugh.

"Thanks, guys. I love you."

"We love you," they say, and we embrace, as a pack.

It's only a moment, but wrapped in their arms, I close my eyes and feel the beat of their hearts, their scents all swirling around me. I feel my feet on the floor—grounded.

That was enough. That was what I needed. We break apart.

"Right," I say, and finally reach for the door handle. I squeeze it once, as if to convince myself it's real.

This moment, each moment, is the only thing I can control. Live in the present, Preston. Make the best of it.

"I'll see you all later," I say, my voice now steadier, and finally walk out of the room, ready to take on whatever comes.

Felix says as the door closes. "Try not to ruin the hair."

CHAPTER 5
Evelyn

Chris continues to exist, which appears to be his main skill set. Time fucking crawls while I wait for Bobby or Tim to come save me from this giant pain in my ass. Every so often, he makes a comment—how cute I am, how I'm holding tension in my shoulders, how I sit too close to my monitor. I respond with increasingly creative threats. He takes it all in stride.

Bobby finally returns, dressed in clothing that doesn't look like a total mess. He addresses me before acknowledging Chris, and I can tell Chris is not used to not being the center of attention.

Ha, sorry, alpha, the world doesn't revolve around you. Even if you are big enough for a gravitational pull.

"Is Tim not back with food?" Bobby asks, looking at his tablet as panic begins to set in on his usually calm persona.

"I'm here," Tim says, rushing in and putting food on my desk—also, not addressing Chris.

"Hi, guys," Chris says, obviously desperate for attention.

They both nod at him and then return their attention to me.

I smirk at him.

Tim, flustered like always, says, "I'm sorry, I got held up. My fob wasn't scanning, and security tried to make me go through the alpha protocol. The guy on duty didn't recognize me."

"Your clothes are on your desk," Bobby says.

Tim unzips his jacket and says, "Thank God. If it weren't for this coat, I probably would have gotten arrested for public indecency with all this cum on me. I'm pretty sure the alpha who ran the restaurant smelled it on me, though."

I grimace at him because...gross.

Bobby removes my salad from the bag and begins assembling it. Just the way I like it. "You should have enough time to eat before your meeting with Preston Geist, but we are on a time crunch."

Bobby finishes assembling my salad and places it in front of me. I stab a few pieces with my fork and am prepared to take that first perfect bite when Chris asks, eyes wide, "You're meeting is with Preston Geist? The actor?"

Bobby looks at me apologetically.

"Yes," I groan and drop my fork. "It hasn't been announced yet, but we are working on a *Torchbearer* game. Please do not let that leave these walls."

His jaw ticks. "Of course."

Oh, strike a nerve, did we? I press. "Please tell me that's not jealousy I hear." I cannot stop my mouth from quirking on the side.

"It's curiosity," he says smoothly.

"Sure it is."

He looks away, pretending to be enthralled by the task of finding his easily findable salads among the five remaining in the bag. His scent, though—steady, a little sharper now—tells a different story.

Typical. Fucking alphas and their jealousy.

Okay, that's the last straw for me with this guy. I want to eat my salad in peace and center myself before my meeting with Preston Geist. I haven't really allowed myself the time to focus on mentally preparing myself for it. And, if I'm being honest with myself, which I recognize I seldom am, I am nervous about the meeting with him. I'm excited to meet a man, an alpha, I might actually call a friend (to whom? I don't know, but that's beside the point). And have I mentioned he's super hot? He's Preston Fucking Geist. I'm trying to repress the inner fangirl, and I don't need some possessive alpha lurking around me right now.

I'm tempted to yell, "Fuck off, you don't own me. Thanks for the cock. Now get the fuck out," but I do still need to treat him like a potential client.

I stab a piece of lettuce a little too aggressively, and my fork punctures the container. "Tim, how about you finish giving Chris your pitch, now that he's...calmed himself?" I say, smirking at Chris. He bristles again, and I think I've found some barbs that bother him; just like me, he's not particularly fond of his inability to completely control his mind and body when his hormones are involved.

Chris tries to protest, "But, I—"

I cut him off. "You can't be in my meeting with Mr. Geist. Not unless you sign a non-disclosure, and seeing as none of our lawyers are here, you can't."

He seems to finally relent. I smirk at him.

I've finally won.

"So, Tim, why don't you take Chris to Conference Room A. The two of you can eat your lunch and go over the pitch. Oh, and show him where he can clean himself up." I give him my most disapproving look and relish the red that appears on his neck in embarrassment. "We'll reconvene after my meeting with Mr. Geist."

Chris doesn't budge. "I want to make sure you eat."

"Chris, I am a grown woman and do not need you to ensure that I eat. Despite your obvious assumptions about omegas and their fitness to thrive, I can feed myself."

"That's not what I—"

I hold my hand up. "You said that you would leave once I ate, and look, I'm eating." I pick up my fork just to end the argument. I take a bite of my salad and chew slowly. I must admit, I appreciate that he is waiting for me to finish chewing before butting in. Most alphas don't exactly give omegas the space to speak. "Now, I need you to leave so I can prepare for this meeting. A meeting that you are not supposed to know about. You have held me up from preparing for it for too long already. After my meeting with Mr. Geist, I will find you and Tim in Conference Room A. I can answer any questions you may have about

Tim's pitch and our proposal then. I'd love it if we could get this deal signed and have it waiting on my lawyer's desk when he comes back after the holiday."

Bobby chimes in, "Your clothes are with Tim's on his desk."

Chris opens his mouth to protest, but I hold up my hand. "And we can discuss this whole...scent-matched pack thing then." I wave him away at the words "pack thing" and turn my attention to my computer, refusing to look at him further.

Out of the corner of my eye, I see Chris turning to Tim for support, practically pleading with him. But he gets none. Tim just gathers his food and says, "Conference Room A is on the other side of the building."

CHAPTER 6
Bob

Evelyn sits with her usual contained fury, stabbing at her greens as if each piece of lettuce has personally offended her. Her voice drops, half-growl. "How dare he think he can tell me what to do. Just because we're supposedly scent aligned."

I sit in the chair in front of her desk and tentatively open my salad. I watch her. The mix of emotion running through her face is evident. She actually does like Chris, but she resents it.

I want to say something reassuring—something like, "It's just chemistry, it doesn't mean anything." But that would be a lie. Scent-alignment does mean something, even if she hates it.

It means something to me, anyway.

I believe him. We are a scent-matched pack, but I don't think Evelyn will ever agree to the idea. Fate. Alphas. They're things she doesn't trust. Especially after her pack left her.

I stab a tomato and try to sound neutral. "At least you didn't get matched with more than one alpha."

She snorts. "Lucky me. One's bad enough."

I want to be in a pack. But, most of all, I want to be with Evelyn. Being in a scent-matched pack with her is literally a dream come true.

But being in a pack with my boss means paperwork. Declarations. Legal acknowledgment that our hormonal cycles are linked enough to affect workplace dynamics. While I waited for the courier to deliver our clothes, I excitedly browsed the company's shared drive for the paperwork. I even started filling out my forms. I've never wanted something so badly.

If she signs the paperwork, it means I get to stay near her without it being unprofessional. It means the company recognizes what I already feel: that I'm built to support her. That my whole nervous system is tuned to the rhythm of her breath. That I am hers—I am her beta.

But she's glaring at her salad, muttering something about being bossed around and how scent-matching is poppycock—burning through her internal thesaurus of "nonsense" synonyms. Every stab of her fork feels like a stab straight to my heart—straight through any hopes I had.

I shouldn't have gotten my hopes up.

I knew it was too good to be true.

I recall the tears that fell from her face when she realized he was the alpha from her past. She felt something—she did—and it wasn't anger. Evelyn hates to feel out of control. This grumbling, this scowling, this denial—it's possible it's all just her way of protecting herself. She's afraid. She feels out of control. It's her feeling like she's falling off a cliff and scrambling, flailing, for a ledge.

I attempt to breach the topic, even though I know the likelihood of it upsetting her is high. But I need to know how she truly feels. And, if I'm being honest, I'm feeling a bit out of control myself. Normally, I know exactly what she needs and wants. But right now, my own feelings are clouding my ability to correctly assess what's going on. I can't tell if my suspicions are true...or just my own desperation flailing for a ledge of hope.

It's best not to let her know how I feel—what I think. Get her to state her opinion.

I clear my throat. "About the HR paperwork," I begin.

She doesn't look up. "Not now."

"Right, of course." I stab a piece of lettuce. Wait a few seconds.

Then, quieter: "It's just—if we are going to do this, we should do it sooner rather than later. The sooner it's documented with HR, the less likely you are to suffer any possible legal ramifications for inappropriate behavior with a subordinate."

She glares at me.

I add, "Not me! I'd never...but, Tim—" More glaring. I gulp. "I don't think he would either, it's just...I want to protect you."

Fuck. I fucked this up.

Her scent flares. I try not to inhale too deeply, but it's impossible.

I guess we won't be filing the pack paperwork, then.

I knew it. I knew it.

Stupid, Bob. Of course, she doesn't want to be in a pack with you.

I bow my head. "Sorry," I murmur. "I didn't mean to—"

She waves me off. "No, it's fine."

I look up, and the scowl on her face softens. She sighs, crosses her arms, and leans back in her chair. She looks at the ceiling, contemplating something, then asks without looking at me, "You believe all this nonsense? That we're a fated pack?"

"No," I say quickly and look down at my salad, desperately trying to stop the tears that are welling in my eyes.

Of course. Of course.

Why would she want to be with you?

She rubs her temple. For a moment, the strong line of her jaw softens. "Bobby. Please don't—" She breaks off, breathing out through her nose. "I just...I hate that this even exists. That people still act like scent bonds are destiny instead of biological noise."

I nod. "Yeah."

I believe it.

At least I thought I did. But that was stupid. I'm stupid.

"Bobby, you're quiet," she says, eyeing me. "You always get quiet when you're trying not to say something."

I feel heat crawl up my neck. "No, I'm just—thinking."

"About?"

The words tumble out before I can stop them. "I know you don't want this, but...it's not all bad, is it? Tim's reliable. The two of you have been friends for a long time. And Chris? I know he's an alpha, but Chris seems really nice. And me—I won't be a bother. Well, no more than I already am. I mean, you already put up with me, right?"

Her eyebrows lift slightly. "Put up with you?"

"Yeah," I say, trying to laugh, "I know I'm...intense sometimes."

"You're dedicated," she corrects.

Dedicated. That's a nice word for hopelessly attached.

She folds her arms, studying me. "You really want this, don't you? To be a pack?"

I freeze. The rational part of me knows this is a question, not a test. The rest of me—the part that has dreamed of this day my whole life—panics.

"Yes," I say. Then, before I can lose the courage, "It's all I've ever wanted. To be part of a pack. To be needed. But, most of all, I want to be your beta. I need to be your beta. Now that I've felt that, if you take it away from me, I...I don't know what I'll do."

My words hang between us, heavier than they should be. I can hear my own pulse in my ears. She doesn't speak for several seconds, and in those seconds, I imagine every version of rejection.

I look at my salad and realize my hand is trembling, barely gripping the fork. *Great. Fucking pathetic.*

Now she's probably going to fire me for being a needy simp. Can you file for unemployment if you're fired for being desperately in love with your boss?

I'll never see her again—

And for what may be the first time since I've known Evelyn, she comforts me. She reaches across the table, grabbing my trembling hand. "Hey." Her voice cuts through the spiral. "Breathe."

I drag in a breath. Her scent wraps around me—steadying, grounding—like it's building a gingerbread house around me, protecting me. Instead of rejecting me, instead of firing me, she squeezes my hand and says, "Bobby. No matter what happens with Chris, you're going to be my beta. Forever."

Cold water splashes over me.

My trembling hands: stop.

The tears I didn't even realize I was spilling: stop.

My heart, my breath, my brain: stop.

I blink. "Really?"

"Yes. We will fill out the paperwork." She pauses, then looks at me, a sly, playful smirk paints her face. "You've earned that much."

The rush of relief is so strong it almost hurts. I want to thank her, but words feel too small. My chest feels too full; my whole body buzzes with the fragile joy of being chosen. Chosen by her.

"Thank you," I manage. "I won't let you down."

"I know," she says simply. "You never do." And the half-smile she quirks isn't laced with her usual annoyance. No, it's almost coy. Like she's hopeful, too. Like she's holding back only because that's what she does. She doesn't let herself show her whole hand. Doesn't let the emotions she thinks make her look weak fully shine through.

But...one day she will. She will...to me. She'll show it to me.

Because I am her beta.

Forever.

We sit in silence again, but it's a different kind now. Her scent has mellowed. My body registers the shift automatically: the faint sweetness that signals rising progesterone. She is my scent-matched mate. It's why I've always been drawn to her. It's how I've always known what she needed. My body was just reacting to her scent subconsciously. It's so hard to ignore, so obvious now, that I can't believe I never saw it before.

Stupid, Bob. Of course, she is your fated mate.

She winces suddenly, pressing a hand to her abdomen.

"Hey," I say, standing quickly. "You okay?"

And I'm at her side before she can mutter, "It's nothing." Her knuckles are white, clenching the fabric of her blazer, when she lets out a defeated laugh. "Just...the usual."

"But...the knot should have been sufficient."

"Tell that to my body." Her tone is light, but the fine tremor in her voice betrays discomfort. My stomach twists with helplessness.

"Do you want me to get Chris?" I ask quietly.

She shakes her head. "No. It'll pass."

Her scent spikes again, faintly sour around the edges—stress pheromones. The scent of pain. It's subtle, but it cuts through me like static.

I glance at the clock. Preston Geist will be here soon.

"It's almost time to meet with Mr. Geist," I remind her softly. "You can't meet with him like this."

"I don't have a choice," she says through gritted teeth. "I can do it. I'll keep the meeting quick."

"But, what if what happened with Chris—"

She gives me a look that would probably vaporize a lesser beta, cutting me off. "I doubt Preston is going to come in claiming we're all scent-matched. I'm fine. I'll be fine. Chris just caught me off guard with that whole 'alpha from my past' thing. It dropped my defenses and got my hormones all out of whack. I'm good now."

I bite my tongue because arguing won't help. Still, the protective instinct rises like a tide, drowning out reason.

Water.

"Let's get you hydrated," I say. "I'll get you some electrolyte water."

Water is all I can offer her. It's not enough, though.

I'm not enough.

I rush to her fridge, get a bottle, and pour it into a glass for her before setting it in front of her. That earns another fleeting smile. She sips it, eyes closed, one hand still on her stomach. The sight makes my chest ache. She's so strong all the time, so determined to outthink her biology—but right now she just looks tired. Defeated.

She doesn't deserve this. She shouldn't have to power through this.

She works so hard. There must be something I can—

Her scent wavers—warm, uneven. My throat tightens with worry. If she has another heat flare while meeting with Preston...he's our most important client. It'll be a disaster. And she'll hate herself for it.

I can't let that happen.

The clock ticks louder. Fifteen minutes now. And that's if he doesn't show up early. She presses her palm harder to her abdomen.

Maybe I can help with more than just hydration.

"You mean it? About me being your beta?" I ask tentatively.

She looks at me in a way that makes me feel like I'm being silly. As if the fact we're meant to be together is as obvious to her as it is to me. "Yes. I do."

"Then...I have a present for you. A Christmas present."

I'm halfway to the door when she adds, "Bobby, you know I don't like Christmas presents."

I pause, hand on the doorframe. "I think you'll like this one."

And before she can argue—before she can tell me not to fuss, not to care too much—I'm already heading for the door, heart pounding.

There's one way this beta can be the alpha she needs.

CHAPTER 7
Evelyn

The worst thing about heat isn't the pain. It's the humiliation—the way your own body betrays you in slow increments until you're a puddle of sweat and desperation and your composure is leaking down your leg.

I try to take another bite of my lunch, but as I bring the fork to my mouth, the lettuce blurs, then dissolves, and another cramp lances through me, blackening my vision and dropping my fork. It's not subtle; my knees buckle under the desk, and my breath shudders out a noise I don't recognize as my own. I grip the edge of the desktop, anchoring myself to something solid, but my hands are slick, and the tremor that shakes me is full-body and unkind.

I just got deep-dicked by the biggest knot I've ever seen—possibly the biggest in the world. What more do you want from me, body!?

Bobby returns, carrying a glossy red gift bag and, I might add, looking far too fucking chipper. "Merry Christmas," he says, while setting the bag on my desk with exaggerated care, as if he's placing a juicy steak at the edge of a tiger cage.

I lean back, stretching my spine until it crackles. My core twinges with a sharp, petulant ache. I scowl, because a) I usually do, b) I'm in fucking pain, and c) I hate Christmas presents.

He pushes the bag an inch closer, then places his hands in his pockets, waiting, avoiding eye contact.

I peel back the tissue with two fingers, peeking in, curiosity actually getting the best of me. Inside is a long, thick, sinuous object swaddled in white: a vibrator, but not just any vibrator. It's pink, glittery, the shaft ridged in smooth, spiraling ripples, and at the base—an unmistakable knot. The kind that's supposed to stretch you so far you forget the bad parts of your day and remember only the blessed, gasping after.

My cheeks are hot, and now my body is acutely aware of itself: the pressure mounting in my abdomen, the way my thighs want to press together. "Bobby," I say, letting the tissue fall back around the toy. "When did you order this?"

He laughs, low and nervous. "The day your black pen had blue ink in it."

"Fuck. I forgot about that abomination."

"Sorry to dredge up old wounds, boss. But the moment you snapped it in half and let out a howl so loud they heard you down in finance, I knew your heat was coming."

Speaking of heat, I can feel it creeping up my neck. The tension is coiling tighter. Bobby's cinnamon is hitting me so hard I can barely think straight. The air around the edges of him is starting to sparkle, as if he's some kind of fuckable, angelic, baked good. I want to eat him, and, not to belabor the point, fuck him.

I pinch the bridge of my nose and try to catalog all the ways I could possibly recover control of the moment, but another cramp hits, sharper this time, and I grip the armrest of my chair just to stay upright.

Bobby notices. Of course he does. He's at my side, rubbing the small of my back the moment my fingers tense. He soothes and hushes and watches me ride out the tremor. When I finally breathe again, he says quietly, "Let me help you, Evelyn."

Not boss. Evelyn.

There's a warmth radiating off him, something beyond pheromones. Something that feels a bit like...love.

"Thank you, Bobby," I say. "For the...gift."

The moment the next cramp hits, doubling me over, Bobby's hand slides beneath my elbow and lifts me from the swivel chair. He lifts me out of the chair like I weigh nothing at all. Bobby's not a large man, but he somehow manages to make me feel small and precious.

"I got you," he murmurs, pulling my head close to his chest and cradling me. He wraps his arms so tightly around me that I nearly melt into him. As the next wave hits, I almost black out, but the sound of his heart beating in my ear, the feel of it beating against my cheek, helps me ride out the wave.

The moment I stop clenching at his shirt, he's behind me, one arm looping around my torso, the other steadying the back of my head.

He bends me forward across the desktop. My skirt rides up, cool air kissing the backs of my thighs, and I manage a hoarse, "Bobby, what the hell—?"

For a moment, I fight him—out of reflex—but then I remember who he is and that these are the safest arms I can be in. He presses me down, face-first onto the desk, as gently as one can manhandle someone.

His palm roams the curve of my back and the swell of my ass as he leans forward, pressing his erection against my backside. "Shh," he says, petting my hair out of my face and kissing my temple. "Easy, baby," he says. "Let me help."

Baby? Did he just fucking call me 'baby'?

Still petting me, he reaches his free hand inside the gift bag. He holds the vibrator up, studying it, twirling it to get a look at the buttons.

The sight of him eyeballing that scandalous thing is so depraved, so sexy, so arousing, I can barely look. I close my eyes, suddenly shy, as if I'm some fair maiden about to be lanced by the pretty boy knight.

I hear the sound before I feel it: the soft whir of a motor, then the sharper buzz of the knot vibrator as he flicks it on. The desperate need within me lights up as if the button he just pressed turns me on, not the vibrator.

"Bobby—" I rasp, and I don't know if it's a plea to stop or a plea to keep going. My voice is shredded, half-gone. I can smell myself, slick and hungry, scent flooding the air with want.

He leans in, lips brushing my ear. "I know exactly what you need, boss."

What happened to 'baby'?

I pout, unable to control it, the neediness in me letting fully loose.

Bobby knows. He always knows. He knows exactly what I want before I even do.

He leans forward, kissing my temple, and I can feel him grin through the kiss. He says, "Oooh, baby, I'm sorry. Don't worry, I know what you want." He calls me "baby" again with a kind of reverence that feels obscene.

I whimper, thrusting my ass against his cock, aching for him to shove something into me.

The vibrator traces a path up my thigh, tickling me. With it, he rides my skirt up higher, and higher, until the vibrator is tracing my ass.

I'm clawing at the desk now, trying to buck into him.

The hand that had been gently pressing me down on the desk is no longer necessary. I'm not going to struggle. I'm not going anywhere. I lift my ass higher as he pushes my skirt above my waist. "You have no idea how many times I imagined you like this. Even more perfect."

He drags the vibrator in lazy, deliberate circles, just barely grazing the edge of my panties, savoring every whimper. When he finally presses the fat head against the damp fabric and lets it vibrate there, against my clit, I wail out, coming so quickly I surprise even myself.

I'm panting, still coming when he deepens his voice and asks, "Do you want my fat knot, baby?"

I pant out, "Yes."

With his free hand, he traces the line of my panties, dipping his fingers in just enough. "So, wet. Is this all for me?"

"Yes."

He shoves my panties down to my knees. I'm soaked, embarrassingly so, and he spends a full minute just rubbing the tip of the vibrator up and down my slit, just barely pressing it into me, then pulling it back.

I can't take it, I need it. I need it inside me. "Please, Bobby. Please fill me with your fat cock."

Finally, he pushes it in and lays his weight against me. He moans against my back, and for a moment, I think it might be his cock entering me, but a buzz spreads through my pelvis, telling me that it's actually not Bobby, but the vibrator. There's no pain, only a tight, beautiful, electric fullness. Bobby rocks his body slowly against me, working it in, pulling it out, working it in, pulling it out, until it's deep in me, hitting the sweet spot deep within my cunt. The knot flares at the base, brushing against my lips. He kisses my cheek, then pushes harder, and the knot enters with a pop. I wail.

"You like that, baby? You like my knot?"

"Yes!"

I clamp down, desperate for friction, desperate for stretch, desperate for fullness, and Bobby obliges. He rocks the shaft in and out, letting the knot pop in incrementally deeper with every thrust. He fondles my breast, pinching my nipple, and with each new place his hand explores, he moans as if he's discovered some new way to bring himself pleasure. He picks up the pace, somehow knowing exactly how much I need: when it's too much; when it's not enough. And just as I'm reaching the edge, thinking it couldn't possibly feel any better, his hand slides down, finding its way to my clit.

"Oh, my God, Evelyn. You're so perfect. You feel so good," he practically growls as his fingers slide and caress, relishing the feel of me. Then he kisses me on the cheek so gently I can barely feel it and says, "You take me so well, babygirl."

Babygirl?

And that was the last piece of the puzzle I needed. A cramp hits, but it's not pain—it's pressure, pure and simple, building at the base of my spine until it explodes in a white-hot shock that leaves me arching against the desk, nails clawing for purchase. I come so hard I see stars, a constellation of them.

Bobby slows slightly, but I scream, "Don't you dare fucking stop," so he keeps fucking the toy into me, relentless, until the aftershocks bleed into another orgasm.

For a moment, I float, suspended in that blank, heavenly void of my brain, brought on by orgasm.

My cheek is mashed against the desk, and I can't muster the energy to peel myself off of it. And for a moment, I think I may be done. I think that may have been sufficient, but then I realize the need is still there. There's a faint, persistent vibration still humming in my core—a sensation that spurs me to start rocking again.

"You need more, baby?" he asks. "It's got a swell function. Do you want my knot locked in you?"

"Yes."

The vibrator clicks, then ramps up to a new, brutal intensity. So does Bobby's thrusting. My thighs are shaking. I'm gasping, drool smeared across the table, and for the first time in years, I don't care how anyone perceives me.

I wail, "Knot me, Bobby," and he obliges.

I barely have time to gasp before the knot at the base inflates, doubling in size, stretching me so wide I see white. It's sudden. It's overwhelming. It's pain, but not the kind of pain you run from. The kind of pain you run toward, pushing through, because you know once you break through the other side, there's nothing but pure animalistic pleasure. The kind of pleasure that runs a giant magnet over the hard dive of your brain, resetting you, making you forget you ever experienced anything else. My body clamps down, milking the knot, and this orgasm hits me like a truck. I scream, hoarse and guttural, letting the pleasure overtake me.

When it's over, I collapse. Legs jelly, fingers trembling, face sticky with sweat.

Bobby tucks a strand of hair behind my ear, wipes the sweat off my cheek with his thumb. "Good girl," he says, and it feels out of place on his breath, but I know he says it for my benefit.

This moment feels like it perfectly encapsulates my permanent inner turmoil: torn between the desire to be a boss and the desire to be a babygirl.

"It has a timer," he whispers. "It should unlock in time for your meeting with Mr. Geist."

My body is a numb, humming mess, but the pain is gone. In its place is a wild, trembling pleasure that still hasn't faded. I'm panting, my chest heaving. I feel like a wild thing recently tamed. I catch my breath just enough to say, "Thank you, Bobby. You take such good care of me."

"No prob, boss."

He remains lying on me, content to pretend he's knotted within me, forgoing his own pleasure. But that's not happening.

It's my turn to take care of him for once.

He looks at me like I'm a work of art. Not broken. Not pathetic. Not something that needs pity. But, perfect. Loved.

I catch my breath, reassemble the bones in my boneless body, and lurch upright. My muscles protest, but I ignore them. This body is going to listen to me for once. I spin on wobbly heels to face him.

"Sit!" I say, voice shot to hell but steady with intent.

He looks at me, shocked and confused.

I take two shuddering steps, then shove him—hard—into my chair. He lands with a thump, arms draped over the armrests, shirt askew, and mouth open in pleasant surprise, as the chair rolls back.

The knot is still inside me, pulsing, locked tight. Every movement makes it shift, sends another ripple through my core. I stand between his knees, hands braced on his shoulders, and grind down.

Bobby's eyes go wide. "You don't have to," he says, voice reverent.

"Shut up," I say, but I'm already reaching for his belt. He's hard—of course he is—straining against the fabric, desperate and pretty. I fumble with the buckle, then with the zipper, and finally I get him free. His cock is flushed and leaking—just for me.

Mine.

I sink to my knees and don't bother teasing; I take him fully in my mouth. He groans—actually groans—like he's never been touched before. The cinnamon is delicious, and I want to taste every last bit of him. I hollow out my cheeks and sink all the way down to the base of his cock, letting him hit the back of my throat. And now he's the one whimpering.

I let him tangle his fingers in my hair, guiding me with careful, tentative pulls, but I set the pace. Slow at first, then faster, until his hips jerk up and I have to dig my nails into his thigh to keep control.

The knot inside me throbs in time with my movements, every suck and swallow echoing back through my own body.

It doesn't take him long, and it's both adorable and flattering. He comes with a stifled gasp, his thighs tightening as if he's trying to hold back, but I don't stop. Not until he's shaking, panting, eyes rolling back in his head.

When I pull off, I look up at him, victorious as I gulp his delicious seed down. He pets my hair back, fixing it, fussing over me like he always does.

I lean forward and rest my head in his lap, and let him grasp my arm and stroke my hair.

He sighs, "I love you, Evelyn."

I look up at him, assessing the truth on his face. "You'd better, or you're fired."

He laughs, "Whatever you say, boss," and I return my head to his lap.

I bring my hand to his knee and close my eyes.

I feel so content. So loved.

And I realize that this feeling isn't just the feeling of being loved. This is love—reciprocated.

I sigh and let myself say it. "I love you, too, Bobby."

CHAPTER 8
Tim

Chris and I bring our lunch into Conference Room A. Chris ducks through the doorway behind me, balancing three salads. I've only got one, which feels slightly embarrassing, like I'm underachieving in the salad department.

Chris chooses the seat at the head of the table, and I settle into the one next to him. Chris opens his three salads all at once and slathers them with multiple cups of Caesar dressing. I open my salad, mix the greens to achieve the perfect distribution of ingredients, and drizzle a small amount of olive oil and vinaigrette over it. He watches me as I combine my oil and vinaigrette with precision. "Why'd you get all that oil if you aren't going to use it?" he asks, pointing at the extra cups.

"They always give me too much," I say, shrugging. I feel judged, though I'm not sure why. Probably because I always feel judged.

The awkward silence settles between us, and I'm not really sure what to talk about. When Chris and I cleaned up and changed our clothes, he kept sneaking glances at me. We brushed against each other more than once in the cramped bathroom and, for a moment, I half expected us just to start fucking against the bathroom sinks. But the moment passed. You'd think all that would have served as a confidence boost, but it probably did the opposite. Now, I'm a nervous wreck, sitting on the edge of my seat just waiting to fuck this all up somehow.

Chris breaks the silence. "So," he says between bites, "Evelyn seems mad at me."

"She's...not mad," I say, which is a lie. "She's just—"

"Annoyed?"

"Profoundly. But always. That's just how she is. Always has been."

He groans, low and rumbly, and I feel it somewhere behind my ribs. "I was trying to help. She looked exhausted."

"She's always exhausted. It's like a hobby."

He snorts.

I glance at him, trying not to stare outright. The man's an architectural wonder—so broad his shirt looks like it's personally offended by how much strain his shoulders put on it. He radiates "protective instincts," the kind that make other alphas bristle, betas like me short-circuit, and omegas bend over.

Well, not all omegas.

"She's independent," I say carefully. "You can't offer to help. She has to ask for it."

"But...she seems hell-bent on not asking."

"That's the game." I stab at a cherry tomato. "You make her think she came up with the idea of being helped."

Chris pauses mid-bite. "That sounds manipulative."

Evelyn's really not much different than the alphas I used to work with at the law firm. She needs to be in control. She needs to feel like anything she does is her choice. While both are driven by ego, I've known Evelyn long enough to realize hers stems from insecurity, while theirs came from a need to dominate.

I shrug again. "It's corporate."

He laughs, and I let myself enjoy the sound. It's the kind of laugh that could ease this anxious beta's worries.

The silence between us is awkward again, but it feels more comfortable; I'm not quite as anxious to fill it. Eventually, we chat for a while about video games, and the topic of superalphas gets broached somehow. I don't quite know, but I think Chris may have directed the conversation in that direction, specifically so he could say: "So, I know I'm not supposed to know, but you're making a *Torchbearer* game? That's really cool."

I smirk at him. Directing the topic like that gives me hope he'll do just fine communicating with Evelyn. "Yep," I say and pop a forkful of lettuce in my mouth, not elaborating, trying to drag the question he really wants to ask out of him.

I can play conversation games, too.

His expression dips, and he asks, "So, she's meeting with Preston Geist? The devastatingly handsome actor?"

"Yep." Another forkful and I watch, wait. He squirms.

"They'll meet in one of these conference rooms?" he looks around as if he's trying to see through the frosted glass into the adjoining rooms.

"No, she'll take him to the Demo Room. It's kind of like a theater."

"Door closed?"

"Usually how meetings work."

He scowls at his salad like it personally offended him and finally says what's on his mind. "He's an alpha."

"Yes." I put my fork down.

"It's not safe for her to be alone with him."

"She's got Bob."

"You've seen that guy, right?"

I laugh before I can stop myself, which feels reckless. My laughter always sounds too loud, too eager, like I'm trying to buy friendship with sound. "Listen, I understand how you feel. I'm not feeling great about it either, but she knows the risks. It's her body. Her company. We have to let her make the choice herself, even if we disagree with it."

He swallows and continues, "Is it wrong that him hurting her isn't what I'm most concerned about?"

"What do you mean?"

"He's a public figure. I wouldn't be surprised if he had even more rut-suppressing hormones running through him than I do just to avoid any bad press. Sure, I'm worried he'll be a danger to her, but, if I'm being honest, I'm most worried that he'll feel...safer."

Preston Geist is incredibly hot, and I know, just from small hints here and there, that Evelyn is incredibly attracted to him—just like everyone. If Preston wanted her, I doubt there'd be much anyone could do to stop the two from getting together. But, instead of fueling Chris's fears with that tidbit of insider info, I ask, "Safer?"

"It's no surprise that I'm kind of a scary guy. Especially to a little thing like her. What if she doesn't think I can protect her as well as he can? What if she doesn't want me? She'd rather be with someone who doesn't tower over her. Someone whose dick isn't as big as her forearm."

I choke on a piece of spinach and can't help but laugh. "You're worried she'll pick him because he has a smaller dick?"

He looks at me in a way that indicates that his massive size and dick are actually a sore spot for him. It's interesting that a man could be insecure about something everyone wishes they had. I try to reassure him. "Hey, you're not scary."

He scoffs.

"Seriously, you're not. You feel...I don't know how to explain it. Solid. Stable. Looming, yeah, but in a protective way. Like you can shield us from all the harshness of the world. Kinda like...a big Christmas tree."

He laughs. "That's just my scent swaying you."

"Maybe, but it doesn't make it less true. If it makes me feel that way, it must be even stronger for Evelyn."

He meets my eyes, and for a second, the air feels heavy, like static before rain. "I still can't believe it's real. I've been looking for so long. I had given up hope. I don't know what I'd do if you were taken away from me."

You?

"You mean her?" I offer.

"No. You. Her. Both of you," he says. "And Bob. He's the packmate I didn't realize I was looking for until I found him."

I look down at my salad to avoid combusting. To have a big, handsome alpha like him talk about wanting to be in a pack with me...it's still hard to believe.

He continues, "I feel like I'm messing everything up with Evelyn," he says. "That I'm going to push her away and lose all of you."

"You're not...well, not irreparably anyway. Not yet."

He nods and says, "Tell me what to do," and pulls out his phone.

"What? Are you going to take notes?"

"Yeah, is that weird?"

"Um...no. I don't think so. Kinda cute actually." I chuckle, enjoying the glimpse I get of the studious Chris who managed to earn so many advanced degrees. Then my face flares with heat as I realize I called him cute.

I poke at my salad, try to cool the heat in my face, and consider my next words. "Well, first, you're overprotective. She doesn't need that."

He starts to protest, but I hold up my fork and say, "You don't get to tell her what she needs, remember. Even if you think she needs it, she doesn't want it."

He nods and types something on his phone.

I wait for him to finish typing and use the moment to take another bite. Once we're both done, I continue, "So, here's the catch-22 of loving Evelyn: she actually really does want to be protected, coddled, treated like a delicate little thing. But she doesn't trust anyone who treats her that way. She suspects ulterior motives. She suspects patronization. So, she won't let anyone do it. You have to figure out how to treat her like she's precious without infantilizing her or stripping away her power."

"Wait...but that doesn't make any sense."

"No shit. That's why I said it was a catch-22." I sigh. "She doesn't want anyone *telling* her she needs protection. But she likes to know someone's in her corner. Quietly. Without making it a performance. There to step in when the boss—and that's the key word here: boss—needs backup."

"Okay, umm...I'm not sure I get it, but...I just need to let her be the one to ask for help, right?"

"Yeah, exactly. The moment she feels like you're trying to make her do something, she's gonna fight you. Present it to her like it's an option. Like you've got it on a platter, are offering it to her, and it's her choice whether or not she takes it."

He nods slowly. "Okay. So I shouldn't storm into the Demo Room while she's with Preston Geist?" He raises his eyebrow and looks for my approval, like this was somehow a genius deduction.

I chuckle. "Definitely not."

He grins sheepishly. "I wasn't planning on it."

I'm not sure if I believe him. I smile and eat another forkful, enjoying the pop of the cherry tomato in my mouth.

Let's put the student to the test.

I swallow and ask, "Okay, imagine this: she's meeting with Preston Geist, demoing the game. What's the best thing you can do?"

He thinks for a second. "Not interrupt."

"Good. And when she comes out?"

"Ask how it went?"

"Yes, but in a casual way. Like, 'How'd it go?' Not 'Did he try anything? Should I throw hands?'"

He nods solemnly. "Casual. Got it. I can be casual."

"You can't," I say. "But I believe in you."

He smirks. "Harsh, but fair."

We chuckle, and then there's silence between us again, but this time it's more comfortable. Like, neither of us feels the need to perform for the other anymore, and we both settle into the joy of our salads. His pine and snow scent shifts, and I can feel he, too, is relaxing—less worried. I steal a glance at him. He's watching me, expression soft, and I feel good—great even. Safe.

But that summons a small panic in me. It's a trait Evelyn and I share: whenever things seem calm and good, that's when we suspect the worst to hit.

I clear my throat and decide to broach the topic that's been weighing on me. "You know, I get how Evelyn feels. This scent-match thing feels too good to be true," I admit. "I keep expecting you to say, 'Oops, Tim shouldn't be in the pack, he's clearly underqualified.'"

"Underqualified?" Chris echoes, incredulous. "You're qualified."

"What do I bring to a pack, though? Betas are supposed to be the calm presence of the pack. There to help calm omegas. But I'm an anxious mess. She has to calm me most of the time. Bob's the one who can calm her. I have nothing to offer."

He leans forward, resting his elbows on the table. "You know what I think?"

"What?"

"I think you don't give yourself enough credit. You can calm her. You can provide that big, safe presence she craves and know exactly how to do it so that she thinks it's her idea. I sensed it earlier. That she trusts you just as much as, if not more than, she trusts Bob. I think you'll be the bridge between us, between Evelyn and me. The one that helps us meet in the middle when the alpha and omega in us clash."

There's that silence again. This time, it's filled with the pulse in my ears.

Chris leans back in his chair, and his expression shifts to something almost...predatory. "You know. I've wanted you for a while."

My pulse jumps. "You—what?"

He shrugs, suddenly shy in a way that's criminally unfair for a man built like a tank. "I liked you. Online, I mean. Before the scent-match thing, before I came here. You were this funny, kind voice. I don't socialize much, so honestly, I'm closer to you than I have been to anyone in a long time."

My chest hurts in that stupid, wonderful way.

He continues. "Your voice on chat. The way you type 'uh' before every serious sentence. You're exactly how I pictured you, just..." His gaze lingers, uncertain. "...more."

My face goes nuclear. "More what?"

He shrugs, smile soft. "Well, definitely bigger."

I throw a crouton at him. It bounces harmlessly off his arm, which, annoyingly, looks like it could deflect bullets. I make a strangled sound somewhere between a laugh and a malfunction. "That's—thank you? I think?"

His elbows are on the table, and the soft light catches in his hair. Everything about him seems too solid for the flimsy chair he's in, like the furniture was never meant to hold that much existence. It's cute how he seems to waffle between having no idea how much space he takes up and being overly aware of it.

I stare down at my salad as my emotions stage a coup. "I—liked you too," I admit, voice small. "But, you know. You were...you. My online friend who was probably way too good for me."

"I'm definitely not too good for you. You know that kiss earlier—that was the first time I've kissed anyone in a long, long time."

My brain replays the moment he kissed me. Evelyn felt so good wrapped around me. I didn't think I could experience anything better. I leaned my head back on the chair, and my eyes caught Chris's: those big, green eyes. Then, without warning, he leaned down and kissed me.

My cock aches at the memory.

He chuckles, shaking his head, and says, voice lower now, "I'm sorry. I shouldn't have done that without asking." He pokes at one of his salads nervously.

I'm starting to understand Chris—his fears. He's afraid that people will see him as a big, scary guy who takes. But he's not. He's a big, cuddly guy who gives.

I open my mouth, close it again, open it. "I didn't...I didn't mind," I admit, voice so quiet it barely exists.

His eyebrows rise. "No?"

I shake my head and titter. "I was surprised."

"Can I fix that?" he asks.

"Fix what?"

"The surprised part."

Before I can answer, he leans over the table—slowly, deliberately—and kisses me again.

It's nothing like the first time. The first was shock; this one is gravity. Warm, certain, gentle. His hand doesn't touch me, but his scent—pine, fresh snow—rolls over me in a wave that makes my brain go blissfully blank.

When he pulls back, I'm still leaning forward like an idiot. My heart stutters. I try to remember how to act like a functional adult, but my brain has reduced itself to looping, *"Oh, no, he's beautiful, you're going to fuck this up, Tim,"* on repeat.

I realize I'm holding my breath. I inhale and, for a moment, I'm weightless. No anxiety, no hierarchy—just pine, snow, cranberries, and pure happiness.

He doesn't look away. That's the worst part. Or maybe the best.

I try to focus on my salad, but my fork's just making tiny craters in the lettuce. I clear my throat, desperate for normalcy. I shake my head, a nervous half-laugh bubbling out. "We should, um, eat our salads before they wilt from romantic tension."

Chris seems totally unbothered, which is offensive because I am actively dying. "Or," he says, "I could suck your dick so you know exactly how much I like you."

I try to say something clever, but all that comes out is a sputter.

CHAPTER 9

I step inside the suffocation box, aka airplane bathroom, and immediately wedge the lever shut. I rip my mask off and toss it in the trash.

There's a second of peace—then I see myself in the mirror and flinch.

Beautiful alpha.

Pretty like an omega. Voice powerful like an alpha. Captivating enough to make anyone do whatever I want.

I should have kept the fucking mask on.

My phone buzzes.

> One dismissal remaining before alpha monitoring authorities are alerted.

I know. I know. I'm fucking trying.

I tap the notification to open the app. I hit "complete," and the app directs me to take a selfie that clearly shows my face and patch on my leg.

I wash my hands until they feel thoroughly scaled and wait for the water to turn off. I pull out an excessive number of paper towels from the dispenser and dry the sink basin. Then pull out even more paper towels to arrange them around the sink area, carefully covering the surface while avoiding my reflection. The plane jolts, so I spread my legs, bracing my feet against the door and toilet, careful not to touch anything with my hands.

So gross. I hate this.

Once I've covered the sink area, I cradle my phone in the sink's basin, hopefully protecting it from any turbulence. I pull the patch and a new mask from my pocket. I cover my face and no longer need to avoid my reflection. This mask has a skull smile, which makes me smile underneath it.

That's better.

I remove the backing from the patch. The disgusting smell of bandage adhesive, combined with a suppressant that is somehow the opposite of my candy cane, makes me want to retch.

I set it on the tiny sink, sticky side up, and slide my joggers down to my knees. I raise the leg of my boxer briefs just enough to see the current patch on my left thigh. My skin is so pale it almost glows under the bad halogen, and the veins ladder up my leg, blue-green. There's a ghost of bruising and skin irritation surrounding my patch.

My cock was half hard, arousal lingering from my dreams of Evelyn when I entered the bathroom, but now I can smell gingerbread. It makes my cock tighten and stand steadfast at attention—as if it's looking for her. I clench my thighs and try to will the erection away.

Is it the mask? Does it have something on it?

I remove my mask and inhale, testing the air. And now I am sure I can smell gingerbread...and cinnamon? My erection swells and pulses, so painfully hard there's no hope of it going down without release.

This phantom gingerbread is just another psychosis, Finn. Your pills will kick in soon, and it will go away.

I can't tell that to my cock, though. It wants her, and it wants her now.

I should take care of this.

I grip my cock hard, squeezing it, angry at it for the annoyance, and close my eyes. As always, when I close my eyes for too long, I see her. Except this time, when I open them, she's still there.

I am not in the plane bathroom anymore. I am standing in Evelyn's glass-walled office. Well, what I imagine is her office, anyway. The lights are dimmed. A man I have imagined to be Bob sits in Evelyn's chair, head lolled back, eyes closed, and he's petting something in his lap.

Where's Evelyn?

I walk around the desk to see Evelyn on the floor, kneeling in front of him, hugging his legs. His cock is flaccid, out of his pants, and she's nuzzling into his thighs.

She looks wrecked. Her blouse and blazer are open, exposing her braless breasts. Her blue skirt is twisted up to her waist, exposing her ass and splayed legs bent underneath her. Her hair is a rat's nest of brown waves, flattened with sweat. Bob is holding her gently, brushing her hair off her brow, but he is looking at nothing. His eyes are unfocused, a little shell-shocked.

I hover, watching them, wishing I could be with her the way he is right now. But I can't. I am an intruder. I am Thanatos, come to spirit her away, except she isn't dying; she's just beautifully, perfectly ruined. *Ruined by someone who isn't me.*

I clutch my chest, trying to will the heartache away.

I need these dreams to stop. I can't take this anymore.

Bob's phone buzzes, and he shifts his weight to get it from his pocket, jostling the dozing Evelyn resting on his lap. "Alright, thank you. You can send him up. Tell him I will greet him in the reception area," he says, then hangs up and returns his phone to his pocket.

Bob looks down at her. "Preston is here."

Evelyn blinks and lifts slightly off his lap; her change in position reveals that she has a vibrator within her. I feel my own cock lurch. I gasp, and she looks right at me.

Did she hear me?

There's a second where I think she's going to scream, but she just squints her eyes as if she's trying to see something far away.

"Hey, boss?" Bob says, returning her attention to him.

Her voice is soft; the harshness it usually holds has melted away. "Yeah, Bobby?"

"Preston is here. I will greet him and wait for you, okay?"

"Yeah, that sounds good," she says, buttoning her shirt and putting herself back together.

"You'll be okay?" Bob asks.

"Yes, go."

Bob hesitates, but she gives him a look so cold and clear he can't refuse. He rolls away from her and stands. He walks out of the room, shoving his cock back into his pants and running his fingers through his hair.

I get closer, and watch her—like always.

The moment he's gone, Evelyn shifts. She's shaking, but she manages to stand upright, the vibrator still locked within her. It must be a knot vibrator. She pulls her skirt down and leans against the desk while she closes her eyes and runs her fingers through her hair. She's not frantic, not really, but I can smell anxiety pluming off of her. She's worried about how she looks as she stands there, unable to move too much, waiting for the vibrator to remove itself from her.

"Don't worry. You look beautiful," I say, assuming she won't hear me.

Her eyes fly open and fix on mine. "Candy Cane?" she asks, voice barely above a whisper.

I freeze.

She heard me? Can she see me?

I want to vanish, but I can't move.

"Candy Cane?" she says again, more pleading, her eyes darting, squinting, searching. "Please say something. I know you're there. I can feel you."

I don't recognize my own voice when I speak. "I'm here."

She startles backward, as if I appear in front of her, then sags, resigned. "God, this fucking heat. Now it's making me hallucinate."

I laugh. "That's funny, considering I'm hallucinating you."

"Well, I don't feel like a hallucination," she says, putting her hands on her hips in defiance.

She's not real, Finn. She's not.

I stay frozen, feeling the entire scene pulse with unreality, my heart pounding in my chest.

She crosses her arms, scrutinizing me. "Who are you?" she asks.

"Thanatos," I say, mocking myself.

She smiles. It's a thin smile that conveys a perpetual state of slight annoyance. A smile that makes you want to grab her by the waist, pull her close, and make the smile curve higher when she feels your cock against her leg. "The god of death? Are you going to ferry me off to the afterlife?"

"I...no. Finn. My name is Finn."

"Finn? Finn Future?"

I clear my throat. "Yes."

"Well, you're early. We're not meant to meet for another few hours." She laughs one loud huffing sound, and the knot vibrator tumbles from her, thudding to the ground. "Fuck," she says and slams her hands on the desk with an angry huff. "Well, it's a good thing I'm hallucinating you, because that would be so embarrassing otherwise. Biggest Fuck Up CEO of the Year Award goes to Evelyn Charles, everybody! This is why you don't let omegas run companies; the horny sluts literally can't keep it in their pants around their clients."

I don't say anything, just watch her, admire her.

She shudders, clutches her side with a low animal noise, then hisses, "God damnit!"

She wobbles, and I reach for her instinctively. My hands close around her arms. She is so warm. I feel the wild, rapid-fire beat of her pulse under my thumb.

I've never been able to touch her before today. She's never been able to see me. She's never heard me, even though I chatter away at her all day.

Why is this happening? Maybe coming to see her was a bad idea. It's obviously making the visions worse.

She presses her face against my neck and inhales, deep. Her gingerbread releases, unsuppressed, needy, and my candy cane reaches out to her, wrapping around her, clawing its way past the chemicals in my body meant to stop it.

Her whole body shudders. "I'm going crazy, aren't I? You can't really be here catching me."

I could lie. But I'm tired, so tired. "I think I'm going crazy, too."

She laughs, and it turns into a whimper as the pain of her heat takes over again.

I pet her hair. It's a stupid instinct, but I do it anyway. She leans into my palm and makes a slight, desperate noise. My body wants to crush her, bite her, drag her under, and never let go, but I force myself to stay gentle.

It's not real. But...I might as well.

"Don't worry, my love," I murmur. "I've been watching you for a long time. I know exactly how you like it."

She whimpers again and clings to me, her fingers white-knuckled on my forearm.

She's a hallucination.

I know it.

I'm crazy.

I know it.

And that's fine. Right now, none of that matters. Right now, she's real, and I'm real, and nothing can stop us. Not my therapist. Not my meds. Not the inner voice that tells me to stay connected to reality.

I'm going to help her. I'm going to be with the woman I love.

I turn her and push her head gently to the desk, the way I know she likes it.

The way I like it.

She arches her back and hitches her skirt up around her hips for me. Her panties are already gone, and her pussy is glistening.

"That's my good girl," I say. "So wet. So pretty."

She glances back over her shoulder, and her mouth is wet and trembling, waiting for me.

God, it's been so long since I've had an omega look at me like that. The thought of any other omega doing it still terrifies me, but on her face, right now, in this moment, I remember why I used to crave it.

I press the head of my cock against her entrance, and she moans. I wait for her to buck back. That's the best part. When you sit right outside, and they can't take it any longer, they thrust back so that you slip inside. *They take. You give.*

The air is hazy, sparkly with the scent of us. I lick the air, gulping down her gingerbread scent. My brain is addled, confused, focused singularly on the point at which my head touches her pussy. And now that the realness has faded, it feels like an actual dream for once. It's a relief, really.

I'm not crazy. I am just dreaming. Thank God.

She whimpers, bucking back, so that I slide into her. When the crest of my head pops through, making her moan in relief, I moan, too.

Mine.

This is the omega I was built to fill.

I slide further into her. She is so slick, so hot. Her muscles seize and clutch around me, desperate for something to hold. I give it to her. The sensation is euphoria, not concentrated on the single point of our contact, but spread through my entirety, waving across my body, carried by every nerve ending whose sole purpose is now to do one thing: experience her.

Fuck her.

Fill her.

Breed her.

Claim her.

I thrust into her the way I've always imagined—hard, fast, relentless, until the sound of her thighs slamming the desk makes my brain foggier—high on the feel of her. A sensation so beautiful, so perfect, I'm single-minded in the pursuit of penetrating her deeper.

I reach around her and stroke her clit the way I know she likes it. Back when I'd watch her old pack rut her, I'd watch her do it herself—desperate for someone to touch her this way, never getting fucked the way she truly wanted.

And she fucking loves it.

With each thrust, when my dick hits that perfect spot within her, and my knot pops past her threshold, she gasps, "Yes!" The rhythm, the melody of her voice—beautiful. I want to make a song out of this so I can play it on a loop for eternity. No song I ever write will ever match the perfection of the one I am playing right now, strumming her clit and drumming her pussy.

She's close, I can feel it in the way she's clenching around me. She's bucking and grunting, making her ass slap against my hips, and sending beautiful waves of undulating flesh down her back. And I'm close, too, my knot swelling to the point where my skin stretches so tight it tugs at my scrotum.

It's time to give her what she wants.

It's time to take what I want.

With my free hand, I press my thumb against her asshole, slick with the same omega need as her perfect pussy. She tightens, spasms, then opens for me, all the resistance melting into need.

She comes so fast, so hard, I think she's going to faint. She squeezes my knot so tight I can barely continue thrusting. She cries, singing in pleasure, singing her praise of my cock.

I knot her, going deep, filling her, stretching her, and it's everything I wanted—her ass against my hips, her cunt milking me for every drop. I lock in, pulse after pulse, filling her until I can't breathe, until I am nothing but an animal. Nothing but a vessel whose sole purpose is to fill this beautiful creature in front of me with his seed.

I lean down and kiss her neck, her ear, her jaw. I want to mark her. Claim her as mine. Force the bond between us to deepen.

What would it hurt? This isn't real, anyway.

But, even in my dreams, I can't bring myself to do something she doesn't want. And the Evelyn I dream of doesn't want to be marked. So I just say, "I wish I could claim you, my love."

She shudders and sighs, then pulls me around so she can hug me. The angle is awkward, but she still manages to hold me so tight I almost lose consciousness.

We lie against the desk in the embrace, relishing the afterglow, as the hypnotic nature of our coupling drops and our scent relents.

When my knot subsides, I pull out of her, slow, not wanting to leave.

The moment my cock is free, the world collapses.

I'm back in the airplane bathroom. My pants are at my knees, my cock is raw and red, and there is semen everywhere. On the walls, the sink, dripping from my hand. I stare at the mess in horror as my consciousness returns, clapping me at the temples and shocking me back to reality.

I scramble to clean, scooping the paper towels I've already laid down and using them to get the rest of the mess. It's too much. It's too fucking much. I've never come this much in my life. Visions of flight attendants walking in, discovering this, having to clean it, sending it to forensics to find the perverted perpetrator, send me into a panic.

Once it's done, and I think I've got it all, I breathe. Relief flooding me. But my heart still pounds in my ears. When I finally have a moment to relax, I pull my pants up and stand trembling over the sink.

How long have I been in here?

I look at my phone. Surprisingly, it avoided the onslaught. It's still on the rut app, requesting the picture of my patch.

Fuck. I almost forgot. I pull my pants back down and snap a picture showing my face and thigh. I don't smile. I hate that this fucking app has so many pictures of my face. The app makes a little confetti animation as I've just achieved something. I close the app and return the phone to my pocket, only for it to buzz in my hand.

Upload failed

My heart stops. Then another:

Connect to wifi or cellular data to sync.

I dismiss it and finally can let myself relax.

I look in the mirror, and for a second, I swear I can see Evelyn standing behind me. Her hair is damp, her blouse buttoned again, but her eyes are glassy, and she's still breathing hard.

"Thanatos," she whispers. "Finn. Are you there?"

I am not crazy.

I am not crazy.

I am not crazy.

But I might be, just a little.

I retrieve my mask, put an extra filter in it, and hide behind it once again. Mask in place, skull smile not quite menacing enough to obscure the face behind it, I unlock the bathroom door and step out.

CHAPTER 10
Chris

Tim does this adorable half-nod, like he's not sure whether to agree or apologize. I stand and tug his chair back, turn it to face me, and rest both palms on his knees. I say, "I've wanted to get a good look at this masterpiece of a cock since I saw you put it in Evelyn earlier."

His face reddens so fast it's flattering. "Jesus, Chris."

I grin and wait for him to stop me, but he doesn't; he just moves his hands to his side and grins stupidly at me, as I sink to my knees. His breath hitches when I nudge his knees further apart with my shoulders.

I pop the button on his pants and watch his face as I slowly pull down the zipper. His legs tense, and his fists clench at his side. And when I reach in, gripping his shaft, he moans, tilting his head back, the same way he did when he entered Evelyn.

I pull his cock from the confines of his pants, and I wasn't exaggerating before; it's a fucking monument. His cock is heavy, the biggest I've seen next to my own, and I'm eager to see if I can take all of him. The moment I take the tip into my mouth, he shudders, and his hands fly to the armrests, gripping them. "Fuck, Chris—" It comes out of him like he didn't mean to say it.

So responsive.

I swirl my tongue around the slit of his cock and watch his knuckles turn white on the armrests. I moan, delighted to taste the cranberries I've dreamed of for most of my life. I bob my head, just the tip at first, getting him wet, making him leak. I look up, keeping eye contact.

Tim's hands hover in the air, hesitant, then finally settle on the sides of my head. He's gentle, like he's afraid I'll break, which is funny considering our size differential.

I go back down, deeper this time, using a hand to jack the part I can't get my mouth around. He's making these tiny, stifled noises, like he's trying not to be overheard.

I swirl my tongue again and suck hard on the head, feeling it pulse against my tongue. "Holy shit," Tim mutters, and his hips jerk. I have to lock my arms to keep him from driving straight down my throat.

My own cock is rock hard, straining in my pants.

"Fuck," he whispers, and I look up. "You're so good at this."

I suck him harder, flattered, intent on blowing his fucking mind. There's a raw satisfaction in reducing this usually soft-spoken nerd to a mess of whimpers and clenched teeth.

He's close; I can feel the tension in his thighs, the way his breath speeds up, the little tremor at the base of his cock. He's about to bust, and I want him to shoot his entire load down my throat. The faint hint of cranberries his precum has provided isn't enough. I want more. I want all of it.

But right as I start jacking him faster, he tugs at my head and says, voice shaky, "Wait. Wait—can I fuck you?"

The words hit me like a shockwave. I pull off with a slurp, wiping my mouth, and look up at him. He looks as surprised as I feel, maybe more.

"Seriously?" I say, grinning.

He nods, desperate and a little terrified. "I want to. Please."

I'm not usually one to be caught off guard, but that rewrites the script so fast I get mental whiplash. For a heartbeat, all I can do is stare at him, mouth open and tongue still tingling from the taste of his cock. His face is flushed, eyes wild with a look that's part terror, part lust, and maybe a dash of "I can't believe I just said that out loud."

I sit back on my heels and run a hand through my hair, feeling a little dizzy from the power exchange. “Don’t get me wrong, I’m game, but we don’t exactly have any lube.”

Tim leans back, grabbing something from among the debris of our lunch. When he turns back to me, he’s holding a little plastic ramekin of olive oil. “Yes, we do,” he says. Then, in a rush, “But if you’d rather, I could just, you know, toss your salad.” He grimaces, afraid to laugh at his own joke and probably afraid I’ll punch him for it.

The corners of my mouth go up involuntarily. “Olive oil actually works. The ancient Greeks and Romans used it. Aristotle even wrote a whole treatise about it. Not that I expect you to have read De Generatione Animalium, but—”

Tim cuts me off, voice firmer now: “That’s fascinating. Can I fuck you now?”

For a moment, all the blood in my body relocates southward. Tim stands, hovering over me and making me actually feel small, here on my knees, looking up at him.

I like this version of him, the version that’s being a bit alpha. I like it a lot.

I push to my feet, looming over him. I could break him in half, and from the look in his eyes, he’d thank me. “Sure, Tiny Tim,” I mock.

He smirks, just a little. “Well, as you already know, I’m not tiny.”

I feel my cheeks heat; he’s caught me off guard yet again, and now I’m envisioning the marvelous cock he’s packing entering me. “Yeah,” I admit. “I know.”

“Can you take it?” he asks, looking to the ground, and I actually fucking blush.

“Yep,” I smirk, trying to exhibit nonchalance and maintain some semblance of power.

He steps closer. “Turn around?” It’s not quite a question, not quite a command.

I do as I’m told. I bend over the conference table and brace my hands against the edge.

Behind me, Tim places a hand on the small of my back. It’s tentative at first, but the next touch is more certain, tracing up my spine, finding the edge of my shirt, and pulling it up to expose skin.

For all his nervous energy, he's gentle, almost reverent. Like he's worried I'll change my mind or laugh at him. I like this version of him, too. The one who is nervous, obviously so, but pushes himself to do what he's afraid of anyway.

I reach under myself, pop the button on my pants. But, before I can even do so myself, he yanks my pants and underwear down. They stop mid-thigh.

I wait for his next move. The anticipation of his touch makes me bite my lip. My cock is killing me. My eagerness is driving it to desperate levels of hard.

Tim pours a little olive oil into his palm, then rubs it between his hands. His hands are warm, slick, as they slide between my cheeks. The sensation of his fingers sliding is so delicious, I lean forward, biting my lip harder.

I hear him exhale, slow and shaky, then he dips a finger into me. The sensation is electric. He's cautious, but not hesitant; he's methodical, working the oil in, stretching me, learning how to open me up. I've bottomed before, but rarely for someone as earnest and focused as this —never for a beta. It's so fucking hot.

I look back, and with his free hand, he's pouring the oil over his cock like some lewd chef. Once the cup is empty, he tosses it back to the table and strokes that gorgeous cock, preparing it for me.

Tim works another finger in, then a third, and I arch my back, pressing into him, wanting more. He's breathing hard, and I can tell doesn't want to wait much longer.

"How much prep do you need?" he asks, voice thin.

"Just go slow," I say. "I can take it."

There's a pause as he pulls his fingers free and lines up the tip of his cock, slick with oil and ambition. He pushes in, slow and careful, and the stretch is fucking glorious.

I groan, loud enough that I worry Evelyn and Bob can hear me down the hall, but not really caring at this point. My fists instinctively slam the table.

Tim fills me, inch by inch, and it's like nothing else—hot, thick, perfect. He bottoms out, hands gripping my hips for dear life.

"Fuck, Chris," he says, awed.

I push back against him. That's all the permission he needs.

He slides in and out with these deliberate, careful strokes. Like he's afraid to go full throttle, afraid to break me, to hurt me, which...no one has ever considered before. I'm large. Unbreakable—at least in their mind. I'm not one to cry while being fucked, but this realization almost makes me.

I'm tempted to tell him to pick up the pace, but it feels so phenomenal, every time I open my mouth to do so, I'm stopped by the wave of pleasure I don't want to ruin.

He pulls out halfway, then drives back in, harder, and I groan. The table shudders under me, and I worry we might break it.

Tim leans over me, bracing himself with a hand on my back, the other palming my ass. He buries his face in my shoulder, panting, lost in sensation. "You feel so fucking good," he whispers, and it's so earnest I almost laugh.

My cock is lying on the table, pre-cum already smearing against the fake wood veneer. I don't stroke it, not yet—I want to draw this out. I like the way Tim's cock fills me, heavy and impossibly thick, the way it brushes against something inside that makes my toes curl.

He starts to move with a little more abandon, hips slamming into my ass, and every slap of skin makes me clench harder around him. The chair on the other side of the table actually rolls back from the force of our collision.

I nearly lose my balance. He's getting bolder, less apologetic, losing himself to the sensation—to the animal. I want him to own it.

"Give it to me," I say, and I push back to meet his thrusts, milking him for all he's worth. The angle's perfect; every time he bottoms out, I see stars.

He reaches around, wraps both hands around my cock, pumping me in rhythm with his hips. My cock swells, the base thickening as my knot forms. Tim's hand finds it, squeezing tentatively, like he's unsure how to handle it.

"I've never been with an alpha before," he says, voice cracking on "alpha" like he's confessing a crush.

"I've never been with a beta before," I manage, fighting not to melt under the dual assault of cock and hand.

"You like it?" Tim breathes.

I nod, can't even get the words out. Instead, I brace my elbows on the table and ride the onslaught.

He squeezes my knot harder, and I gasp.

He keeps fucking me, the pace growing wild, ragged. I can feel the sweat drip down my back, hear the squelch of olive oil and the slap of skin. His hand is slick on my cock, and every time his thumb brushes the crown, I have to dig my nails into the table to keep from howling.

The pressure builds, molten and unstoppable. I arch my back, Tim slams forward, and he squeezes my knot so hard, I blow my load all over the conference table, thick ropes spattering across the surface.

"Oh, God," Tim moans, and his cock twitches inside me, then releases a hot rush. As he comes, his pulls me closer to his hips like he's afraid I'll bolt. The sudden fullness triggers a second, smaller orgasm in me. When the wave ends, I collapse against the table, sweating and panting and completely ruined.

He pulls out, and the loss is almost as good as the penetration itself. I twist to stand up, pulling my pants back to my waist, and catch Tim staring at the mess I made.

"Holy fuck," he says, voice still trembling.

"Yeah," I say.

He laughs, and it's the most unguarded sound I've ever heard from him. He tucks himself away, zips up, and then awkwardly pulls me into a hug.

It surprises me. I wasn't expecting it, but I suppose with him I should have. I like the feel of his arms around me and the way he nuzzles into my neck.

"You okay?" he asks, suddenly shy again.

"Better than okay," I say, almost choking up. No one I've ever been with has asked how I was after they bottomed me. No one's ever hugged me after either. Usually, it's a "thanks, bro" or some other toxically-alpha phrase derived from the conviction that they can't show tenderness or care for anyone that isn't an omega.

So, this is why you get a beta.

I kiss him on the forehead.

He blushes, but he doesn't let go. He asks, "Do you want to see my silly game idea now?"

"It's not silly," I correct. "It has emotional resonance."

He flushes. "I—thank you. So, you were listening?"

"Yeah, I was on the cusp of rutting, but I was definitely listening...mostly. Show me the pitch."

"Okay, let's get cleaned up first, though."

CHAPTER 11
Preston

The office is thirty percent glass, seventy percent concrete, and one hundred percent empty, or so it seems as I tug open the main doors. My reflection doubles and triples in the layered glass walls ahead of me as I cross the marbled floor. Each version of me looks increasingly unsure. Cameras track my movement, and I almost feel like I'm on a set.

Smile.

I approach what I suppose is a security desk, even though there is no guard on duty. A robotic voice comes out of the kiosk saying, "Welcome, Preston Geist. Please approach the retina scanner." I scan my eye, and the kiosk says, "Identity verified. Please scan the QR code in your *SuppDose* app to verify you are up-to-date on your suppressants. A note signed by a licensed physician will also be accepted, but will need manual verification. Please expect delays of..." It pauses for a long moment. My heart sinks as I think it's broken, but the voice finally returns. "Two thousand five hundred three minutes for manual verification."

My heart sinks again when I can't find my phone.

Calm the fuck down, Pres. Just take it one moment at a time. Stop panicking over everything.

It's in my other pocket. I breathe, steadying my hands, and scan the

QR code from the app. After a few seconds, it says, "Verified" and plays a tune, blowing a load of digital confetti.

Oh, that's cute. Why does this make me feel better somehow?

The closest glass door ahead opens, and a nearby screen blinks on. A man appears on the screen saying, "When you hear the countdown—holy crap! Preston Geist! Whoa, big day!"

I smile and say, "Hiya!" placing my hands in my pockets to hide their shaking.

"Oh, my God, are they making a *Torchbearer* game!?"

I put my finger to my mouth exaggeratedly. "Now, that sounds like something that would be under NDA if it were true."

"Understood, sir, no worries, I can keep my mouth shut. Um...can I tell my omega that I met you, though? She loves your movies."

"Sure, keep it in the pack," I wink, and I try not to show how this exchange exhausts me.

His eyes light up when he says, "Thank you," and even though these types of public performances have gotten harder for me, I do still really love the look on a fan's face when you do something to make them happy.

Still grinning, the remote guard ushers me through a dance of doors and countdowns until I am standing in front of the elevator. I scan its edges and can't find any buttons.

The guard, now on a monitor above the elevator, says, "I'll send you right to the floor. They'll be waiting for you there."

"Okay, great!"

"It was great to meet you. Happy holidays!"

I remove my hands from my pockets and turn up the charm. "Yeah, you, too! Hold on a sec. How big's your pack?"

He looks confused. "There's six of us."

"Whoa, lucky guy. You know Bob? The admin here?"

He nods.

"Send him an email with your address. I'll send six tickets to a launch party we have next month. All expenses paid."

"Wow, I'm...they're gonna freak. Thank you, sir," he says right as the elevator doors open.

"Happy holidays."

"You, too!" he beams. And right before he closes out the video feed, he turns his head and says, "You guys will not believe this!"

Either he works from home, or he's already spilling the beans.

Oh, well. I'll let PR know—see if we want to do a contained leak. Marketing wanted to start teasing it, anyway.

The elevator is one of those perfectly silent, frictionless deals that you wouldn't know was moving if it weren't for the fact that your stomach feels like it jolts into your balls. Inside, I watch myself in the mirrored walls. I look...alright. My crew—my pack—did as good a job as anyone could, making me look like I'm still a movie star. I smooth my hair back, feeling the calm before the storm.

Oh, fuck! What was I going to say when I first saw her!?

Lines, Pres!? Lines!?

At floor thirty-seven, the doors whisper open to an empty reception area. It's so quiet I feel like I've stumbled into a post-apocalyptic zombie movie: no distant chatter, no sound of phones. I step out and let the doors close behind me.

Creepy.

There's a large desk where I presume a receptionist should be sitting, but all I see is a tablet that says, "Welcome, Preston Geist."

Is...is the tablet the welcome party?

I look left, then right, consider texting Bob, then decide that walking forward with confidence is preferable to standing around like a lost child.

I step left when a door to my right opens. Bob emerges chugging from a water bottle, his shirt half untucked, and his hair sticking up in the back. He smells faintly of cinnamon and gingerbread, and I wonder if he's just come from some Christmas party. Every time I've ever seen him, he's looked so put together. It's like this version of him is catfishing me with dishevelment.

"Mr. Geist!" Bob beams, returning the cap to his water bottle. "Evelyn will be here in just a moment." He's breathless as he tucks his shirt in and straightens his hair. "It's wonderful to finally meet you in person."

"Yeah, you, too," I reply, trying not to sound disappointed. He's not who I came here to see, after all.

"Water?" he asks, retrieving a bottle from behind the reception desk for me.

I accept it with thanks and try not to chug it, but my throat feels like it's closing up.

We make small talk, and I'm doing my best to be a showman, but everything I say comes out flat. I'm hyper-aware of my own body, my own skin, and the way the air feels different here, more alive. Acting is an art. And acting well is an art of...disassociation isn't quite the word, but you have to lose yourself. It has to be automatic. You can't be thinking about every word, every movement. But something other than my anxiety has my brain disconnected from my body. Everything is a conscious effort, and everything is slightly delayed. My brain says "speak," my body says "buffering," then it performs the command.

Time seems to lose all meaning. The water in my hand is like a lifeline. I'm sipping it too frequently just to prove to myself I'm real.

Wait? Is there something in this water?

Bob glances back at the door he came from, turning my attention to it. There's a faint, spicy warmth leaking through the seal of the door, and the air in front of it starts to thicken somehow. Efficient, close-cadenced footsteps approach—each one sending a pulse through the air that radiates through me.

She's coming.

There's a pause at the threshold. My hands twitch in my pockets. I try not to hold my breath, but of course I do. The woman I've been obsessed with for a year is on the other side of that door.

And then, she's there: Evelyn Charles, my omega.

The sight of her knocks me out of whatever daze I've been in for the last few minutes. My senses that were dulling are now hyper-attuned to her.

'Beautiful' is a fucking understatement.

She's in a blue suit with a skirt cut perfectly to just above the knee. It's a power suit by definition. Made for her body and not ostentatious, but indicates wealth and authority. It's tailored to amplify her hourglass shape. It makes me want to wrap my arms around her waist and inhale her, then let go, stand back, and let her punch me in my face for my audacity.

Her hair is down in a way that, until today, I have never seen. Usually, it's up in an unassuming bun, one that says, "I don't have time to cater to your alpha gaze bullshit; I've got a business to run and balls to bust."

Her makeup is so subtle it looks as if she barely had time to put it on, but she's got the skin of someone who barely needs it. She's glowing. She smells faintly of gingerbread and pine and some clean, cool thing—like snow outside a bakery.

I'm not prepared. No one is, probably—not for a woman who can make a tailored navy skirt suit look like it was designed for a coveted goddess covertly disguised as a CEO.

She pauses, letting the door close behind her, and looks at me. Her eyes do this quick scan; she's sizing me up. She smiles, then walks forward. The faint click of her heels hitting the marble punctuates the moment, speeding up the beat of my heart.

She extends a hand for a shake, which is unexpected even though it is the professional thing to do. I almost fucking whimper at the sight of her reaching toward me.

Before I remove my hands from my pockets, I palm my rut patch, barely feeling it through the layers of clothing, just to make sure it's in place. I take a step forward and almost trip over my own feet in my haste to touch her. Then, I hesitate, just a moment, as I overthink the shake. *Is it a power shake? A greeting shake? Am I supposed to squeeze or let her lead?* I give her what I hope is a normal-person handshake, but she smiles wider, and I know instantly I got the pressure wrong.

My brain, treacherous, files this interaction away for future sleepless nights of self-flagellation.

Jesus Christ, Pres. You're a grown man. Get it together.

"Thank you for coming on such short notice, Preston," she says, voice brisk but not unkind. "Especially on a holiday."

Preston? Are we on a first-name basis now?

"My pleasure," I say, and try to calibrate how much of a smile is professional but not desperate. I probably overshoot. "Nice to meet you in person, finally." Then I add, testing it, to see how she reacts, "Evelyn."

A smile quirks the corner of her lips.

"I owe you an apology," she says, spreading her hands, "for the technical issues earlier today."

I shake my head, fighting the urge to break eye contact. "It's cool. Happens to the best of us. I've always wondered what this place looked like, anyway."

Evelyn laughs, but then she studies me, her head tilted. "Would you like a quick tour of the office on the way to the Demo Room?"

"That'd be great."

She says to Bob, but her eyes remain on me, "Bob, would you mind preparing the Demo Room for us?"

Bob flinches, as if he didn't expect her to ask this of him, but is the ever dutiful assistant. "Sure," he says, "I'll have the build ready for you when you arrive."

She winks at him. "You always know exactly what I need, Bobby." Then, to me: "Shall we?"

Bob exits through the door they came through, but she leads me through the one on the opposite side of the reception area.

The office is a mostly open floor plan, but it's peppered with glass corridors and offices, partitioning the floor into other large open spaces. No one else is here, so the deeper recesses are darkened, but the lights are motion-activated, flickering on as we move. The large windows surrounding the space light up the area well enough for me to see the rows upon rows of desks, all decorated with various personal items. The snow falling in the background somehow adds to the post-apocalyptic vibe.

"This is the main development floor." Then, gesturing to the right, she says, "And over there is the QA department."

Her pace is quick, but not rushed, and I follow her as if it's what my feet were designed to do. Evelyn walks confidently, swaying her hips in a way that is so seductive, I think I might be hypnotized. We fall into step, the two of us, and it feels like I'm a puppet on a string, being dragged along by my puppeteer.

CHAPTER 12
Tim

It's hard to keep a straight face when your alpha is making goo-goo eyes at you over the glow of a slide deck projected on a screen shorter than he is, especially when your own brain is still oozing endorphins from the orgasms you gave each other approximately seventeen minutes ago.

I try to focus on the bullet points. It would be easier if Chris didn't keep stretching, thigh muscles rippling under his expensive pants, like he wants to show me exactly where my jaw should drop.

Chris's hand is on his chin, index finger pressed to his lips, pensive and a little predatory. He's not a bad guy, but he's an alpha in the same way wild tigers are cats: good at pretending to be domesticated, until they're not. We both know he wants to jump me again, right here in the conference room. His scent spikes every time I turn my back to him, practically screaming, "I want to tear that ass up."

And the fact that I can smell it doesn't help either, because each time I catch a whiff of that protective pine and cooling snow, I think, *Fuck, I can't believe I'm so lucky to be in a pack.* And not letting myself go down a spiral of excitement and disbelief takes considerable willpower.

Each slide I show him is a steady circle jerk of reasons he should choose us for this project, but they're unnecessary at this point. I don't really think they ever were necessary—he only considered doing this as a favor to me. That thought also almost sends me down a spiral, wondering: *how I could be so lucky to have such a good friend?* and *why I was so stupid to be so nervous*?

I get to the slide concerning the overall projected costs and potential timelines. Chris whistles. "That's a lot of money."

I glance at him, and maybe it's the lingering post-orgasm confidence, or maybe it's the way his scent is telling me, "It'll all be okay," but I let slip: "You can afford it."

His smile blooms slowly, like a sunrise of smug satisfaction. "Don't get cocky," he says, eyes flicking down to my crotch and back up again. "I was going to agree no matter what, but you can at least pretend I'm a typical client."

We chuckle quietly to each other. I prepare to lob an equally flirty line when there's a sound on the other side of the conference room door: high heels, staccato and determined against the tiled floor outside.

I freeze.

Chris's nostrils flare, and suddenly his game face is on, all warmth gone, replaced by an intense, animal focus. I've only seen this look on him in videos from his old pro-gaming days.

Videos I definitely haven't masturbated to. Definitely not.

Then comes the gingerbread-tinted scent leaking through the seams of the door and sending an electric zing through us.

She's not alone, either. There's a male voice punctuating the sharp clap of heels. It's too enticing, too suave, too...*simpy?*

Chris stands, nearly upending his chair, all alpha instincts dialed to eleven. He's forgotten the pitch, and his whole body is laser-focused on Evelyn, and, who I assume is, Preston Geist. I'm not sure what Chris is planning, but whatever it is, it's messy. His gaze flickers backward to me, and I can't tell if he's daring me to stop him or asking me to. Either way, I gotta stop him. Hopefully, I don't get my ass handed to me first.

I'm in front of him faster than I thought possible, instinct overriding anxiety. "Don't," I say, a hand out, firm. He stops, surprised that I dared to intercept him and, probably more surprised, that he actually listened. The glare he cuts me makes me instantly regret having put any authority into that word, but it's too late. The moment hangs in the air, thick.

The glass walls of Conference Room A are frosted, providing privacy for confidential meetings, but I make out a blur of Evelyn's blue blazer and a burgundy-clad presence at her side. Chris's eyes track the movement, his jaw clenched so hard I can hear the molars grinding.

Chris fucking growls, and I'm so intimidated I almost cower.

Is he going to bark at me?

My cranberry scent spills out of me, tinged with submission, and Chris stands taller, spurred by the display, and his pine fills the room, asserting its dominance.

Evelyn, right outside the room, stops talking for a moment. She must sense the showdown in the room, her omega nostrils able to smell us through the walls. Her gingerbread spikes, angry, protective, with that alpha-like flare that says, "Touch my beta and die, and also, don't fucking tell me what to do!" Chris doesn't notice, or if he does, he's misreading it. His alpha bias assumes the flare from Evelyn signals she needs help, when I, knowing Evelyn, understand it means, "I'm about to make your life a living hell if you don't calm the fuck down."

I have to stop him. I can't let him go out there, even if he kills me in the process.

"Sit down," I hiss, yanking him back by the sleeve. "If you go out there right now, she is going to hate you forever."

He looks at me, eyes wild, but I see the logic land. He glances at me, then back at the frosted wall, visibly calculating, visibly trying to throttle back the hormones raging within him. It's kind of impressive, actually.

I try to return to normalcy, try to distract him, by advancing the slide and saying, "So about the revenue split—"

Chris interrupts, "We have to go out there. Now." His voice is low but urgent, as he grips the top of the chair he's refusing to sit back down in. It's like he's physically holding himself back with it.

Fat lot of good shackling yourself to a rolling chair is going to do. It certainly can't stop you.

I try to put as much power behind my voice as possible and say, "We have to stay here," emphasizing "have."

Chris leans in, voice dropped to a deadly whisper. "We have to do something."

"Like what?" I keep my gaze on the slide, but my hands are shaking, and I practically have to staple them to the table. "Stage a dramatic rescue from a hallway conversation?"

"Yes. We have to save her."

"Save her from what?" I snap. "Doing her job?"

He gives me a look of utter disbelief, like I've missed the punchline to a joke that's been set up for years. "She's in heat." He says it so simply, like it's a universally recognized crisis, and I'm a fucking idiot for not knowing. "That's not pre-heat, Tim. That's full heat. And Preston Geist can smell it, too."

Of course, he can smell it. I can smell it, and I'm a beta on the other side of a wall. The air is so saturated with gingerbread, you'd think I was an employee at Santa's fucking workshop. It's making my skull fizz and my skin itch.

I grit my teeth, determined not to be one of those weak-willed betas who do whatever an alpha tells them to.

Chris, on the other hand, has released his chair and is now pacing behind it. His breath is shallow, haunted. It's almost comical. He looks like a hungry dog drooling outside a bakery window, trying to figure out how to break in.

He lets out a rumble, low and soft. "She shouldn't be alone with him when she's in heat."

I need to get him to chill the hell out. I can see from the way his hands are fisting that he's seconds away from hurling his body through the glass walls to pummel Preston Geist.

"Chris," I say, pitched low and serious. The same tone I use with Evelyn when she's about to go ballistic about something. The same tone I'd use if I encountered a bear in the woods. "If you go out there right now, she will never accept you as a packmate. Never." I let that sink in.

His pacing freezes, and he snaps his attention to me. His breath heaves his chest. And the hint of snow, usually overpowered by strong, stable, pine, picks up. It glitters around him, as if he were physically emitting snowflakes. And that's when I realize that this display isn't aggression. It's not anger. This isn't a big, scary alpha ready to tear the world down. It's a little boy trapped in a big man's body, terrified of losing what he loves. Desperate to run to it and hug it, hold it tight so it won't leave him.

I make my voice even more gentle. "Please, Chris. Listen to me. I've known Evelyn most of my life. I know that she will never accept this scent-matched thing with a guy who tries to act like he knows what's best for her."

Something in him crumples. He collapses back into his chair, deflated. The tension in the air doesn't drop so much as vibrate at a higher, angrier frequency. Chris, like Evelyn, can't stand to not be in control.

"Fine," he growls, "but that talentless hack is going to try something. You know that, right?" He rakes a hand through his hair, grips his head, elbows on the table, staring at the surface unblinking.

"Can you smell if he is rutting?" I ask.

Chris looks up and blinks as if his mind is catching up. His nostrils flare as his body runs a diagnostic on the air. His eyes go distant, then sharp again. Confusion or realization softens his face when she says, "Actually, no."

"See?" I say, keeping my voice annoyingly calm. "You're the only one about to make a scene. His suppressants are working better than yours, so maybe take a page from his pharmacy and chill."

Chris blinks, considering my words, and logic breaks through the hormone haze. "He's not rutting," he admits reluctantly. "He's just... there."

"Exactly. His suppressants actually work, unlike someone else's," I say, eyebrows raised. "So, sit there, pretend you want to hear this pitch, and then maybe tell your endocrinologist to up your dosage."

He sighs, defeated, and says, "Fiiiiine." He folds his arms on the table and sinks his face to them, nestling his head in the embrace of his arms as if he's going to nap or perhaps cry.

CHAPTER 13
Preston

I nod, trying to pay attention, but my eyes keep drifting back to Evelyn. I can't help but focus on the subtle sway of her hips or the way her hair falls across her shoulders. There's a desk with multiple bobbleheads of popular video game characters behind her right now, and instead of focusing on her words, all I can think about is how their heads would wobble if I bent her over the desk and rutted into her.

My patch is doing some heavy fucking lifting right now, and I'm grateful it's there—helping me keep my shit together.

Thank you, Derek.

We round a corner, revealing a wall of posters showcasing games her company has produced.

There's so many!

"Impressive," I murmur, stepping closer to one of them, studying the detailed background. "You have quite the portfolio."

"Thank you. We're very proud of the work we've done," Evelyn says, moving to stand beside me. Her arm brushes against mine, and a shiver runs through me at the brief contact.

I turn to look at her, emboldened. "I'd expect nothing less from a woman who's so impressive herself."

Her eyes widen slightly, but then a slow, seductive smile spreads across her lips. "You think I'm impressive?"

"Extremely," I say with a gulp, as her eyes rake me.

"Is that so?" She smirks and trails a finger down my arm, stopping my heart.

Holy shit.

She tilts her head at me. "And what exactly do you find impressive about me, Preston?" Evelyn asks playfully, her voice low and sultry, but there's something almost predatory in the question. Like she's testing me. Like a viper waiting to strike. If I provide the wrong answer, I get the fangs. If I provide the right one, I get swallowed whole.

I gulp, my heart pounding. I try to keep my voice steady and say, "Everything. Your beauty, your grace—"

Her smile drops just a little, as if she's now forcing it, and she backs away just a hint. The shift is barely noticeable, but I pick it up quickly enough to change tactics. I continue, "Your power, your brilliance, your vision, your discipline, the way you command a room, and...the way you don't take anyone's shit."

Her smile is real again, and she leans closer to me.

She inhales, drawing in my scent. My subtle hot chocolate is trying its damnedest to escape the confines of my over-medicated body and rush to her. My rut may be suppressed, but my dick is certainly not.

She thinks for a moment, and the vibe shifts again. She chuckles to herself, then steps in even closer until our bodies are nearly touching. She's back on the attack. "Yeah, but it's nothing compared to the beauty and grace, right?" She presses forward, nearly pinning me to the wall. "You like all those other things, but only because they present a challenge. You'd love to break it out of me, show everyone how powerful you are by getting me to submit to your whims, huh?"

A nervous laugh escapes me. "Absolutely not."

"Sure," my beautiful viper hisses.

My breath hitches. "Evelyn, you are the most captivating, terrifying creature I have ever met. I don't want to tame you. I want to be worthy of your attention."

A slow, sensual smile spreads across her lips. "Is that so?"

I nod, emboldened by her reaction. "Absolutely. Evelyn, I don't want you to submit to my whims. In fact, I would gladly submit to your every whim and command."

Her eyes darken with desire, and she steps even closer, until our bodies are nearly flush. I can feel the heat radiating off her skin. And the scent that was subtle, repressed by my patch, is now intoxicating, penetrating my pores: it's sweet and beautiful, dominated by gingerbread but with hints of cinnamon, cranberries, and pine. I'm drowning in her, utterly entranced.

She tilts her head, considering me with a heated gaze. "Are you saying you want me to dominate you, alpha?" she purrs. "To make you submit completely to my will?"

I breathe, hardly able to believe this is happening. I nod eagerly, barely able to form words. "Yes, Evelyn. Please. I'm yours to command."

A wicked gleam enters her eyes, and she leans in until her lips are a mere breath from mine. I tremble with anticipation, desperate to close the distance and claim her mouth.

But then, abruptly, she pulls back. I blink in confusion as reality crashes back in.

What was I thinking, propositioning her like this? We barely know each other. I came to her place of business and threw myself at her feet, like some desperate horn dog. *Who does that?*

Evelyn clears her throat and straightens her blazer, her eyes darting away for a moment. "Let's continue the tour, shall we?"

What just happened? I stare at her for a moment, stunned by her abrupt shift in demeanor. I nod mutely, trying to get my racing heart under control. One minute, we were flirting shamelessly; the next, she's all business again. *Did I misread her signals that badly?*

Fucking stupid, Preston.

You can't just throw yourself at the feet of someone like her. She has better things to do than play with you.

She begins to walk away, but I need to know what happened. I need to fix this. I need to apologize. I can't let the moment end like that. Taking a chance, I reach out and gently grasp her wrist. "Evelyn, wait. Please."

She pauses and looks at my hand around her wrist. Her calm business facade covers a snarl I can't see, but can somehow sense. I let go.

I take a deep breath. "Evelyn, please forgive my forwardness. From the moment you took control of that first conference call, you have consumed my thoughts. Every time we've spoken, I've tried to muster up the courage to ask you out. I let my excitement and desperation get the better of me."

Her eyes widen in surprise at my bold confession. For a moment, she seems at a loss for words. She lurches forward, attacks, poking me in the chest with her forefinger. "Quite bold of you to grab me like that, Preston. Especially with my seven-foot alpha right behind that door." She nods towards a conference room, her voice rising slightly as if she wants to be overheard.

Seven-foot alpha?

Shit. I'm dead.

The mingling of various scents on her suddenly makes sense.

Shit, I would have understood that if it weren't for this fucking rut patch.

Thanks, a-fucking-lot, Derek*!*

Evelyn steps closer, her finger still firmly in place on my sternum. She leans in, her breath hot against my ear as she whispers seductively, "I think we should go to the Demo Room. I can show you the game you came here to see." She drags a finger down my chest, sending shock-waves to my crotch. She drifts lower and lower until she's below my waistband. Then slowly, forcefully, she cups the front of my trousers, pressing against my rock-hard cock.

I inhale sharply.

She says, "And I'll show you what you really want in there."

I'm frozen, paralyzed by the venom of her power and beauty, fully unable to speak.

She yanks my tie, lurching me toward her, pressing her nose to my neck, inhaling. Then her tongue lies flat against my skin, tracing upward, making me fucking whimper.

"Mmm, hot chocolate," she purrs approvingly.

For a moment, I'm embarrassed by my sweet, chocolatey scent. An alpha shouldn't smell like a dessert. But Evelyn inhales deeply, a look of pure hunger in her eyes, and I realize she's into it. Really into it.

The scent of aroused omega, like fresh gingerbread, intensifies. She's in heat. I'm hit with a wave of lust so powerful it nearly brings me to my knees. My patch, no longer able to stop this.

God, I want her. I've never wanted anyone or anything so badly in my life. But I have my wits about me enough to know that having sex with her in her office, especially with her huge alpha lurking around, isn't exactly the smartest thing I could do.

"Evelyn," I groan, my voice rough with need. "Are you sure about this? What about your alpha?"

She smirks wickedly. "Oh, he's not really my alpha. He just thinks he is." Her hand squeezes me through my trousers, and I nearly buckle.

"Lead the way then," I manage to say. I'll follow her anywhere at this point. Honestly, he can kill me; I don't really care anymore.

Evelyn sashays down the hall, an extra sway in her hips that has me hypnotized. She pauses outside a door marked "Demo Room" and throws a coy look over her shoulder.

"Ready to play, Preston?" she purrs.

I walk behind her, returning the confidence to my step, adjusting my tie, and my hair. "You have no idea how ready."

CHAPTER 14
Evelyn

I drag Preston through the door by his stupidly soft and expensive sleeve. The fabric is so velvety that it makes me want to bite him. He tries to plant his feet, but I'm small and mean and more determined than he is.

I'm still reeling a bit from that ridiculous hallucination I had earlier. Like, I get it, I'm in pre-heat. But hallucinating that a ghost who looked like Zain from Fate's Five, that boy band I used to be obsessed with, fucked me silly after claiming to be the client I'm meeting with later: that's a new one for me. Maybe my dads were right about tapering off suppressants not being as effective as I hoped.

Anyway, time to fuck Preston.

The Demo Room is a bastardization of a home theater. Three rows of reclining seats face a big-ass flatscreen, with so many consoles and devices plugged into it I suspect a Fire Marshall would have something to say about it.

Bobby's standing at the front of the room, back hunched, controller slack in his hand, while he fiddles with various settings on the panel of switches that control the whole thing. *Torchbearer*'s title screen plays on the TV; it's deeply emotional music blares through the surround sound and hits me in the chest.

Bobby looks up when we stumble in. His nostrils flare just a little, taking me in, then Preston, then the fact that I am clutching Preston's wrist like a leash. His heavy sigh is barely audible over the music.

"Uh," Bobby says, eyeing us. "Hey, boss."

Preston opens his mouth, but I squeeze his wrist, and he snaps it shut. "Sit," I say, pointing at the front row.

Preston sits.

Good boy.

I eye fuck the two of them only for a moment, then head to the door, clicking the lock. Bobby sets the controller down. Preston is looking between the two of us as if he's star-struck, which is funny, because he's the movie star.

It's so fucking hot in here.

I yank my blazer off and let it fall to the floor, then start on the buttons of my blouse.

Neither of them says a word.

When I hit the last button, I shrug the blouse off and let it slide down my arms. My skin prickles in the cold air, but I'm still burning up.

Preston's eyes are wide and wet, locked on my bare breasts. His mouth is actually hanging open. I want to yell at him, but I'm not sure what for, so instead I fumble with the zipper on my skirt.

Bobby coughs, a polite little noise. "Should I—uh—"

"You stay." My skirt puddles around my feet. I step out of it and kick it aside.

Preston is not breathing. His pupils are so blown that his irises are just a rim of blue.

I hook my thumbs into the waistband of my panties, make eye contact with him, and say, "Is this what you came to see, Preston?"

He makes a noise—an honest-to-god whimper. "Yes," he says. "Oh, God, yes."

I've always found Preston sexy. Fuck, everyone does. But that whimper nearly undoes me. I roll the underwear down my legs, slow and methodical, and watch them both squirm.

Bobby doesn't look away; he doesn't even twitch when I turn to him and say, "You good, Bob?" He knows I mean business when I call him Bob.

He nods, eyes on my face. "Of course, Evelyn."

Another good boy. Ready to do what he's told.

Preston tries to stand, probably to get closer, but I hold up a hand. He freezes.

"Don't get ahead of yourself," I say, stepping down the aisle until I'm within arm's reach. I plant myself in front of Preston, legs apart, hands on my hips.

I hate that he looks so good. I hate that I want to let him do whatever he wants to me. I hate that part of myself so much: the part that wants to bend over and lift her ass for a handsome face with an alpha scent. But instead of doing all that, I say, "You want me so bad, you can fucking ask for it."

He blinks, speechless. Then: "Evelyn, I—"

"Yes or no?"

He swallows hard. "Yes. Please."

I quirk my eyebrow at him. "That's not asking."

"Evelyn, may I please taste you?"

I stifle a whimper because, *holy fucking shit, Preston Geist, Hottest Man Alive 2012, is asking to lick my pussy. It's not 2012, but he's still so fucking hot. And delicious.*

I reach out, take his tie in my fist, and yank him forward until his mouth is at my navel. He doesn't resist, just breathes deep. The heat on his cheeks and the heat of his breath on my navel spike my scent. My arousal drips down my leg. He looks up, smiling with teeth that probably cost more than all the electronics in this room combined, and waits.

I thread my fingers through his soft hair. "So beautiful," I say, admiring his face. "I'm going to fuck that pretty face now, okay?" He nods, grin widening, and I pull his face closer.

Preston kisses my stomach, open-mouthed and reverent, then lowers his tongue, dragging it over the skin above my hipbone. He falls to his knees at my feet and grips my ass. Then his mouth finally finds its target. When his tongue traces up my slit, lapping me up, I feel the full-body jolt of it, like electricity connecting us. And when he gets to my clit with a quick flick, I can't help but coo, "Such a good boy."

I look to Bobby, still standing beside the television, silently awaiting my orders.

"Stop watching," I nearly yell.

Bobby's lip twitches, and he says, confused, "You asked me to stay."

I reach behind me, snap my fingers, pointing at the ground. "Stop watching and come here."

Bobby moves behind me; his hands are gentle when they brush my shoulder. He trails soft kisses against my neck.

Preston pulls my clit into a suck and moans into me, tongue insistent and greedy. I can't help grinding against his face. I look down and see the top of his head, hair already mussed, and I want to shove him all the way inside me and never let go.

Bobby's hands drift lower, circling my waist, thumbs stroking little arcs against my skin. "Tell me what you want, boss," he murmurs.

I glare at him, but the effect is ruined by the way I'm already panting. "I want you to teach him how to please me," I say.

Bobby's eyes glint. "Consider it done." Without a sound, he sinks to his knees beside Preston and grabs his hair, gentle but firm, pulling his head back. Preston looks up, face slick, lips red, breathing hard, eyes almost wild with need.

"You want to fuck her?" Bobby says, the question is so casual it could be about the weather.

Preston nods.

"Then you have to earn it. Follow my lead." He guides Preston's head back between my legs, and I gasp as the tongue returns, more desperate than before. Bobby kneels in front of me, kisses my navel, the curve of my hip, the inside of my thigh. He doesn't compete with Preston—he coordinates, and it's unfair how good they are together when their tongues are both between my folds.

Every nerve ending is raw. Every thought is static.

I can't stay upright. I push them away, and they look at me, doe-eyed and dutiful. I fall into the seat I had pushed Preston into and spread my legs wide so that they can fit between my thighs. Preston grabs my knees, spreading them to their brink. He makes this hungry, wordless noise that is somehow more pathetic, more desperate than a whimper. It's as if he might die if he doesn't return his mouth to my pussy.

Bobby strokes my ankle, murmurs, "That's it, boss. Let go," as he kisses his way back up my legs to join Preston.

I close my eyes and do exactly that. One of them, both of them, I don't know, puts his fingers inside me, and I hear Bobby whisper, "Right there is where she likes it." The pressure increases, and as the perfect spot within me is prodded and poked.

The orgasm hits so fast I don't even recognize it as pleasure until I'm gasping, shuddering, wailing. Preston doesn't stop, even when I try to push him away, and Bobby holds my foot steady while I ride it out.

When I finally stop coming, Preston is staring up at me, looking fucked-out and lost. Bobby wipes the corner of his mouth, presses a soft kiss on my hip, and then stands, pulling me to my feet.

I'm not done, though. I need more.

"I'm going to fuck you now," I say, breathless to Preston. "Sit."

Preston looks like he's about to pass out, but he manages to fumble his fly open, cock already hard. Then sits back in the chair. I climb into his lap, arms around his neck, and line him up. As I lower on his length, I pull his hair back and admire his beautiful, perfect face, then close my eyes and admire the beautiful, perfect stretch.

He smiles, slack-jawed, blissed out, eyes half closed, and almost lets out a gleeful laugh as I sink as far as I can. I've taken him fully into me, but want him closer. I wrap my arms around him, pull him tight, and try to meld our bodies into one perfect wintery snack. He does the same, squeezing me so tight that neither of us can move. I suck at the gland on his neck and love the pleasured moans it brings out of him. I sing in my head, *I'm fucking a movie star.*

Ha, wait until I tell Styles about this. She's going to lose it.

I grind my hips, slow, then rough, making sure that famous cock rolls against every square inch.

Bobby stands behind me and grabs both of my tits, squeezing and kneading as I grind harder and harder. He places one of my breasts in Preston's mouth, who eagerly sucks. Bobby leans in, kisses my ear, and whispers, "He doesn't deserve you."

"I know," I grunt back.

Preston's hands dig into my hips. He thrusts up, sloppy and frantic, and I bite his collarbone, not hard enough to leave a mark, but just enough to tell him that he's mine.

Fucking delicious.

I lick my lips. The bite breaks something in Preston. Not the skin, but a dam that was holding back his scent. It has been muted up to this point, but now it rises to an intensity that matches my own. Together they're thick, warping the air as they combine—as if they too are fucking, becoming one. Gingerbread and hot chocolate: a perfect treat for a cold day like today. It just needs...a sprinkle of cinnamon.

I turn, grab Bobby by the collar, and yank him down for a kiss.

Delicious.

Bobby kisses back, hard, and slides one hand down between Preston and me. His fingers find my clit and circle it, slow and steady, not stopping even when I whimper.

Preston lasts exactly eight seconds after that. His knot swells as he locks into me. He moans, hips bucking, and comes so hard I nearly lose my balance. Bobby keeps working me, relentlessly, and I come again, pulling Preston by the hair into a deep kiss.

Preston reclines the seat back, and I collapse onto him, panting. He wraps his arms around me, hugging me. Bobby reclines in the seat beside us and reaches across, petting my head, the way he knows I like.

I close my eyes and breathe, feeling satiated and full.

"Fuck, that bite almost fully overrode my rut patch," Preston pants. "I was hoping to take you to dinner, I wasn't expecting to be knot locked with you before you even showed me the game."

I open my eyes, and the *Torchbearer* title screen is still on the screen, waiting for us to play. "I'm sorry, Preston. That was wholly unprofessional of me," I say, nuzzling my cheek into the fabric of his suit. It's lovely and soft. I like it. It feels good against my face. "I'll show you the game once your knot deflates."

Bobby laughs. He wipes sweat from my brow and kisses the top of my head. "Boss, will you please admit you're in heat now?"

I grin, despite myself. "It's pre-heat, Bobby. I've just always wanted to fuck Preston."

"Flattered," Preston says.

"Shut up."

CHAPTER 15

Chris

I step out of the uncomfortably over-warm Conference Room A. Tim trails after me, trying to stop me, but I need to get out of there. The scent of us is getting to be too much, and I need some air.

He's jittery, which isn't new, but is more pronounced now. "We should just wait for her in there," he says, the confidence from earlier waning.

"I can't breathe in there. It's too hot," I say, walking forward, loosening my tie. "You said she has fans in her office? Let's wait in there for her."

He nods and sticks close to my side, which is kind of cute. "She did say she'd find us in—"

"I'm sure she won't mind." I wrap my arm around his shoulders. "You said the contract was in her office, right? We'll go in there, I'll cool off, I'll sign the papers, and we'll wait. No big deal."

I suspect it might actually be a really big deal to Evelyn. I know I'm pushing it, but the idea of being caged up in that room for one more second makes me want to hurl my body through every fucking glass wall in this goddamn office.

I know it's just the alpha hormones making me want to put one less wall between me and Evelyn. *And that fucking blond phony who's trying to steal my girl.*

I know.

But I'm trying to convince Tim and myself otherwise.

I attempt to distract Tim with official business talk. "She'll sign the deal, right?" I ask.

Tim shoots me a glance and offers a tight smile. "Yeah, she'll sign."

I release him and continue walking toward her office. "Let's go make you Creative Director, yeah?"

He smiles, small, as if getting too excited will cause the whole thing to fall through.

I want to bring up that we'll also be in a pack, but I don't, because, honestly, that feels a bit tenuous right now.

Tim accidentally let slip that the highest-tier funding option would be the biggest deal they've ever struck. So, of course, I had to choose that one. *So what if it eats into my retirement?* I'm hoping the fact that I'll be financing the biggest project the studio has ever signed, *bigger than the one Preston Fucking Geist is currently funding, I might add,* will make Evelyn more willing to talk with me about being a scent-match pack. I'm trying not to think too hard about whether that is financially manipulative.

We round the corner and can see Evelyn's office. The door is open, and the blinds on the glass walls are all drawn.

Bob stumbles out.

He's sweating, his hair a mess, and his clothes are in a state of half-dressed disarray. And, in his hand, like a grotesque Olympic torch, is an enormous knot vibrator. A fucking huge one. Like...so huge it makes me feel ways I don't often feel.

Outmatched. Small. Unnecessary.

Bob freezes when he sees us.

Tim is the first to react. "Uh, hey, Bob."

Bob's eyes flick from Tim to me and then back. "Oh, uh, hey." He's got the look of someone who just got off a roller coaster, but is rushing back to ride again.

A second passes. I stare at him.

"She's in the Demo Room with Preston Geist, isn't she?" I ask.

"No," Bob says, but he's a terrible liar.

"Let me guess," I say, "you three are fucking in the Demo Room."

Bob opens his mouth, closes it, tries again. "It's...not like that."

"You have a giant knot vibrator in your hand, Bob."

He looks down, as if he's just noticed it. "Oh, shit," he says, and tries to hide it behind his back, which only makes it more visible.

Tim snorts, and I feel a bit betrayed by the amusement on his face.

Well, fuck. There goes my resolve to stay away from the Demo Room.

I clench my fists and say, "I'm going to the Demo Room."

Tim says, "Chris, please don't—"

I need an excuse.

"I just need her to sign this paperwork," I say, already moving. I rush into her office and realize that I have no idea where the fuck the paperwork is. I scan the room. Bob and Tim stand at the door. I can't tell if they're trying to block me in, but it wouldn't really matter either way. It won't stop me.

I spot a manila folder on her desk and rush to it. I hold it up to them. "This it?"

"Um, I'm not sure," Bob says, obviously lying again.

I inspect the folder, careful not to open it just in case, and spot my name on the cover. "Yep, this is it," I say. I snatch a pen from a cup and storm to the door.

I gotta say. I respect how long they stand their ground. It's admirable, really. Bob, the tiny thing, actually stands longer, and I think he would have let me barrel right into him, but once Tim bailed, so did his resolve.

Tim says, meekly, defeated, as I walk away from them, "Chris, this isn't a good—"

"Sorry, Tim, I have paperwork," I say over my shoulder, speed walking in the direction of the Demo Room, led by my nose and cock, "I need her to sign."

Bob jogs up and tries to intercept me. "She's really not going to like—"

"I'm not afraid of her," I say, which might be a lie. "I'm just going to get her signature. This is business. She'll understand."

I shove Bob out of my way and am relieved when he doesn't fall. I'll apologize for that after I murder Preston Geist for daring to even look at my omega.

The Demo Room is at the end of a hall, tucked behind a glass door plastered with a cartoon fox mascot. The light is on inside, bleeding through the closed blinds of the glass walls.

I grab the handle. The door is locked. *Of course.*

I'm going to fucking rip his dick off.

I knock. And say as sweetly as I can manage through gritted teeth, "Evelyn. Open up."

A muffled "go away" comes from inside.

The anger in me is so red-hot, I have to stifle a roar.

Breath. Breath, Chris. You can control this. You are not a hormone-fueled monster.

Tim and Bob are behind me, flanking me like doomed wingmen.

I knock again, harder. I unclench my teeth. And I say so gently, like I'm *a tiger* trying to coax a baby deer into my den *so I can rip its fucking throat out,* "Evelyn, it's Chris. We need to talk."

Silence, then a loud bang—something knocked over.

What was that? If he's hurting her, I'm gonna...well, I'm gonna kill him, regardless.

I look at the handle, then at Bob. "I don't suppose you have a key?"

He hesitates. "I, um, left it in there."

Another lie.

Tim says, "She's not going to be happy if you storm in there, Chris."

I grip the handle and give it a test rattle. It's a flimsy thing, meant to keep out beta office workers and cleaning crews, not seven-foot, brick house alphas.

Fuck it.

I brace, plant my foot just so, and kick under the handle, avoiding the glass. The frame shudders and pops; the door swings open.

The first thing I see is a TV displaying a 3D model of Torchbearer running through a city. The second thing I see is Preston Geist, sitting in a theater chair at the front of the room, controller in hand, eyes glued to the screen. He looks over his shoulder at us with all the nonchalance of a movie star.

Shit. They're just demoing the game. Evelyn mentioned the NDA... and Fuck.

And that's when I see the third thing: Evelyn, kneeling in front of Preston, mouth around his cock, one hand curled around the base, the other gripping his thigh, completely naked. She hasn't even looked up.

Bob ducks past me, still gripping the knot vibrator, then tries to slink to the far side of the room, as if he's hoping no one will see him.

Tim stands frozen, mouth open.

I take a breath, count to three, and say, "Evelyn. We need your signature."

Preston grins at me and asks, "Can it wait?" His voice is weirdly steady.

I want to knock out every one of those perfect, pearly white teeth.

Evelyn pops off Preston's cock and wipes her mouth with the back of her hand. "Is my signature really why you came storming in here, Chris?" Her voice is steady, but I can see her nostrils flaring against the effort it takes not to bare her teeth.

"Yes," I say, convincing no one.

She stands and stretches, elongating her beautiful naked body. Her and Preston Geist's scents are fogging the place, dizzying me, and making her look like some ethereal goddess.

I swoon. She glares.

I compose myself, shift my erection in my pants, and continue, "I'm eager to get this deal signed. Earlier today, I thought you were eager to, as well."

She smirks—no, sneers. "So you broke into the room for a signature? Typical alpha."

I ignore the jab. "Just sign the paperwork, Evelyn."

She saunters toward me, slow and unhurried. And now I'm realizing that I'm the baby deer and I just stumbled into a dragon's den.

She snatches the pen from my hand and bends over a table by the door. Her ass is pointed at me, and I can see her perfect, glistening pussy. Her gingerbread flares, angry, almost pelting me in the gut, as she scrawls her name.

When she's done, she turns quickly, and the inertia of the move makes her tits bounce. I pretend not to notice when she shoves the folder back at me, hitting me in the chest with it. "Happy?"

"Ecstatic," I say, palming the folder to my chest. When my fingers brush hers, for a moment, I think that'll be the end of the fight. That she'll feel the love in my touch and forgive me. Of course, I'm not so lucky, because she snatches her hand away, appalled.

"Is there anything else you want from me, Chris?" she says, hissing my name out like it's a curse.

I...hadn't really thought this whole thing through.

"I want you." I nod to Bob and Tim, who are both pretending to find the floor endlessly fascinating. "And them."

She doesn't flinch, doesn't give an inch. She steps past me, close enough that the gingerbread punch of her heat nearly buckles my knees. "What if I don't want any of you?" she says. "Did any of you fucking think of that? I don't recall you ever asking me what I want."

"But—"

"You don't own me, Chris," Evelyn says. Her tone is razor sharp, perfectly even, a scalpel making the first incision. "Or them." She looks at Bob and Tim, then right back at me, unblinking. Her eyes shine with something between fury and exhaustion.

I hesitate, mouth dry. "I didn't say—"

"You didn't have to." She folds her arms against her chest. "Breaking down my fucking door; disrespecting me, Preston, my fucking NDA—that all says you think you own me and can do with me whatever you want."

Bob slinks next to Preston and slides into the adjacent chair, practically hiding behind him.

Has Bob chosen a new alpha, too?

Tim just...exists—frozen behind Evelyn, not breathing.

I want to say something sweet, something perfect, like a beta love interest in a movie. Something that makes all this better. Something that explains precisely how I feel and how terrified I am of losing her. Something that makes her forgive me for letting my hormones get the best of me. But most of all, something that makes her realize we're destined to be together. But what comes out is, "We're a scent-matched pack, Evelyn."

She laughs. "Scent-matching is a fairy tale. We're a group of emotionally stunted adults. Some of whom get paid to make video games," she says, gesturing at her, Tim, and Bob. "Some of whom fuck in Demo Rooms." She points a finger at Preston, who does not look remotely ashamed. "And some of whom," she gestures at me, "think the world is a Christmas romcom movie." She moves closer and stabs me in the chest with her finger, where I still grip the envelope. "And now that I've signed that, you and I are business partners. That's it. Nothing more."

She turns her back to me and strolls toward Preston. "Preston, I'm sorry. We'll need to continue this some other time." She takes the controller from Preston, flicks off the television with her thumb, then drops the controller onto the nearby table like it's somehow more repulsive to her than I am.

"Evelyn, I—"

"I'm not going to do this with you, Chris. Not here. Not now."

I have to keep my hands from shaking.

Fuck, she's infuriating.

My tone deepens, threatening a bark, "Then when? Then where, Evelyn? I—"

She shouts, cutting me off, "Don't you dare bark at me!" Her nostrils flare, jaw tight.

I soften my tone and plead, "Evelyn. Please. I have looked for you my whole life. I can't lose you again. I need you."

Her eyes go soft for a split second, then snap back to projecting pure fury. "You need me?!" she mocks. "But you haven't for a moment asked what I need. You think you know what I need. You think I need you. But I don't. I have Bobby. I have Tim. And the two of them and that knot vibrator will be more than sufficient. I'm fucking tired of alphas deciding what my life is going to be."

"Evelyn, I love y—"

"Don't." She holds up her hand, stopping me, then unleashes another verbal assault. "What if I want to be loved and respected for who I am and what I can do, not because I'm a fucking omega and you finally found a place that you can fit that huge fucking cock. I fucking hate alphas. All you're good for is a fucking knot and a headache."

She winces slightly, hand on her side, a cramp obviously overtaking her. I rush to her, and she hisses at me, "Don't you fucking dare touch me."

She walks toward Preston and Bob, signals for them to rise, and they do. They hover beside her, not quite blocking her from me, but obviously ready to throw themselves in front of her if necessary.

I stand, petrified, unsure what to do. I look at Tim, hoping for assistance. He just shakes his head and says, "Dude, I told you not to touch that door," and walks to join them.

And he did tell me. He warned me this exact thing would happen.

She crosses her arms, now flanked by a pack she seems to be choosing that doesn't include me, and says, "You were wrong about us. We are not fated. We are simply..." She thinks for a moment and finishes with, "nostalgic."

I do not like being told I am wrong.

I am not wrong. She is my mate.

But I am also not an idiot. I can see it in her posture—the calculations, the clawed wildcat of her will. Her confident nudity. If I press her now, she'll just dig in deeper, and I'll lose her.

Again.

So I back off and try to remember my notes from earlier.

"I'm sorry," I say, looking at the ground.

Evelyn raises her brows, pure skepticism. "Did you just apologize?"

I nod. "Yes. I am sorry. You're right—I didn't ask what you wanted." I let the silence hang.

She looks at me for a long second, as if peering into my skull for an off-switch. Then, and only then, does she seem to let her shoulders relax. "Good," she says.

She's panting and trying very hard not to let anyone see that she's in pain. She's fighting not just me, but a pain boiling within her.

I want to ask if she's okay, but that would be the habitual mistake. She doesn't want my pity. She doesn't want my sympathy. She wants my respect. And I can tell by the way her heat is flaring that, as much as she thinks she hates me right now, she actually does what my cock.

I kneel and ask, "Evelyn, what is it that you want me to do?"

The smile that quirks on her lips is all the confirmation I need: she does want me.

CHAPTER 16
Bob

It seems like the big oaf is finally getting it. You'd think a smart man like him would have figured this out by now, given everything Tim and I have already told him, but I suppose all those alpha hormones addle the brain when an omega is in heat, especially a scent-matched one.

She wants Chris. It's apparent to everyone with a nose. The air is thick with gingerbread, hot chocolate, pine, cranberries, and cinnamon. She wants all of us, but only on her terms. She needs to be in control—even when she's losing it.

Everyone else is still stuck in the drama of the moment. All I can think about, though, is how much it must suck to have your whole body betray you and then have to keep up this "icy bitch CEO" facade for an audience that includes two employees, two clients, and a knot vibrator.

Evelyn presses her palm against her waist, fingers splayed, knuckles white, and moseys toward Chris. "Oh, so now you care what I want?" she says, pinning Chris with that look she saves for people who try to mansplain her own game to her.

Chris bows his head in a way that looks like deference if you're feeling generous or like a whipped dog if you're not. "Yes," he says, voice sanded down to nothing. "I do."

She rolls her eyes and immediately winces. "Goddamn it." She's doubled over, rage-red. "Fucking...argh."

Chris reaches toward her, but she slices the air with her free hand. "Don't," she hisses, and the effect is so intense he literally freezes, hand hanging mid-air.

Tim, who's currently behind me like I'm some kind of body shield, mutters, "Her heat is getting worse."

Preston is radiating that weirdly zen self-assurance alphas tend to have after they just had an omega's mouth wrapped around their dick. But he leans back, perches himself against a chair, feigning nonchalance, and catches my eye. He lifts an eyebrow, darting his eye to Evelyn, like, "What should we do?"

He's asking me?

Evelyn stands in front of Chris, breathing like she's running a marathon. She clutches her side, scent spiking in waves so thick you could surf them. Still standing, but barely. So, I go to her.

Somehow, Preston beats me there, and Tim follows in my wake, shoulder-hunched but determined. Chris remains frozen in his holding pattern, all that alpha energy funneled into his clenched jaw.

Preston pulls a bottle of water out of nowhere and says, "Drink some water."

She wheezes, "Stop fucking telling me what to do!" and knocks it clear out of his hand.

Preston has yet to be schooled in the ways of Evelyn: the omega tortured by her desire to be in charge while simultaneously being coddled.

"Boss," I say, crouching down and putting a hand on her back. "Would you like some water?" I ask.

You can't tell her. You gotta ask her.

She doesn't shrug me off. Instead, she leans into the touch, just a millimeter, but it's progress.

I cut Preston a glance, hoping he gets the memo. He nods.

Looks like this alpha can simp with the rest of us.

I nod to Tim. He finds another water bottle, holding it in her general vicinity.

She snatches it, downs half in a single gulp, then throws her head back and howls. Not a wolf howl—a banshee scream of frustration, heat, and flesh-tearing pain. She drops the bottle, wipes her mouth, and glares at Chris with murder in her eyes.

"Are you proud of yourself?" she says. "Was this your master plan? Trigger my heat by knocking down the door with your bullshit alpha hormones?"

Chris's voice is barely a whisper. "No," he says, "but if you need—"

"What I need," she snaps, "is for everyone to stop treating me like I'm going to fall apart if I don't get knotted every ten minutes." She waves at the room with her free hand, the gesture encompassing us all as if she's grouping us in with this idiot. "I am fine."

Preston slinks to her side, all lean muscle and Hollywood teeth. He leans in, whispering something in her ear. Whatever it is, it makes her shiver, not with fear but with this raw, hungry wanting.

The gingerbread is so thick now that it coats my tongue, but under it, there's a zing of hot chocolate and snow.

Preston whispers something else, and she giggles. She actually fucking giggles, and I think maybe I might have some things to learn from him.

Preston backs away slightly, grinning like a madman. I look at him, dumbfounded, and whisper, "What did you say?"

He grins, shoulders me, and smooths his hair. "Just wait. You'll see."

"Okay," she says finally, breathless and raw. "Fine. If you all want to make yourselves useful, then do it. But on my terms. Understood?"

We all nod.

She locks eyes with Chris, waiting for him to say something stupid, but to his credit, he keeps his mouth shut.

Then she looks away, sets her jaw. Her knees are shaking. Preston puts an arm around her waist. She lets him.

The change in her is sudden, disorienting, as if she's a coin showing her other side. She leans into him, strokes his jacket, and says, "This is nice. So soft. You have good taste." She nuzzles her face against it.

He says, "My stylist has good taste. I had a whole team prepare me to meet you."

She melts a little, but his grip keeps her upright. "You got dressed up just for me?"

"Of course."

She smiles, small and flattered, then remembers herself. She commands, "Take me over there."

He obliges and helps her walk to the table at the back of the room. She sweeps the controllers and various papers aside and leans over, palms flat on the surface.

She turns to me, to Preston, to Tim, and the look in her eyes is pure challenge. "You three," she says, "are going to fuck me so hard I forget my own name." She looks back at Chris. "And you are going to sit there and watch. You're going to see what it looks like when someone actually listens to me."

Chris makes a strangled sound, but doesn't move.

I'm the first to respond. "You got it, boss," I say, which makes Tim snort and Preston give this little half-bow like he's on a stage.

Preston is the closest, so he slides up behind her, hands ghosting over her hips, one palm flattening on her back to pin her. He's taller than she is by a foot, and the way he bends to her is both predatory and reverent. "This what you want?" he murmurs, lips close to her ear.

She doesn't answer, just leans onto her elbows and lifts her ass higher, glaring at Chris the whole time. Preston presses against her, sliding through her slick but not yet entering her.

Tim circles to her side, kissing her shoulders, her neck, her cheeks. With each kiss, she melts a little more, the tension, anger, and pain leaving her. Tim whispers, "God, Evie. You're so beautiful." When he says that, the fight in her eyes drains, and she looks like she may cry.

I'm on the other side, petting her back and kissing her ear. I stroke her jaw, put myself between her gaze and Chris, the source of her anger, and say, "You are. You're so beautiful, baby."

She nuzzles into my palm, coating it with tears that refuse to fall. It breaks my fucking heart that she feels she has to fight this side of herself, just like she has to fight the rest of the world. I whisper, "Oh, baby, you want us to take care of you?"

She bites her lip and nods.

I hold her face between my palms and kiss her so deeply that it feels like she may suck the life out of me. "Don't worry, baby, we're going to make it all better."

Preston is sliding between her legs, rubbing her clit with his cock. I nod to him. He takes the cue, pulls back slightly, lines up, and presses in. Evelyn breathes in with a hiss, and her body tenses again. He gives her a second to adjust, then starts to move, slow at first, but building. She doesn't make another sound except for these half-choked breaths, like she's daring herself not to give him the satisfaction.

Her hand reaches between her legs, and Tim whispers, "Let us do that for you, Evie." She nods, returning her elbows to the table, body still taught, but relaxing a little.

Tim, Preston, and I slide our hands down her front, and when our hands all meet at her soaked clit, I catch Preston's eyes. He grins, and suddenly I realize: *I've been fucking a movie star.* I blush and turn my sights back on Evelyn.

Tim kneels by her head, strokes her hair, whispers to her. "It's okay, Evie. We're going to take such good care of you. The pain will stop soon, okay?" She lowers to the table, less tense, trying to relax, but she still won't let herself. "Evelyn, I love you so much. Let go. We won't let you fall. Bob and I, we got you no matter what. Just like always, right?" She nods and lets him kiss her, and she finally relaxes, lying against the table, feet no longer bracing her against the floor.

Preston stops thrusting, leans forward, and whispers, "Want me to hold you while I knot you, babygirl?" *This guy is a quick learner.* She nods. "I got you. Come here," he coos, turning her around and wrapping her arms around his neck and lifting her into his arms. He sits on the edge of the table, bringing her to his lap and slowly sinking her onto his dick. Preston grips her ass and rocks her gently, just barely popping his knot in and out of her.

She's not content for long. She braces her knees against the table, gains leverage, and tries to lift up and down on him. Preston grips her ass more firmly, stopping her. She glares at him for just a moment, her mouth purses as if it's loading up a "Fuck you, Preston! Let go of me!" But before she can bite his head off, he whispers, "Baby, you work so hard all the time. Let us do our job." For a moment, I think she may continue to fight him, but she doesn't. She relaxes, wraps her legs around him, and lets him bring her head to his chest.

Preston kisses the top of her head and says, "That's it. That's my good girl." She moans, low, so deep, you'd think her uterus finally relaxed and let that moan out. He returns his hands to her ass so that he can move her slowly up and down his cock.

Tim and I pet her head and back, kiss her, rub her clit in that firm, circular motion I've learned she loves. We all whisper her praises as the scent of gingerbread and hot chocolate wraps us in a warm, comforting embrace.

"You're taking him so well."

"Oh, babygirl, you feel so good."

"I love you."

"What a good girl."

It's dizzying, almost sleep-inducing, as if this is all just some beautiful, relaxing dream. Evelyn whimpers, nuzzles into Preston's chest, pants, then lets out another deep wail as she comes.

Preston moans. "Does that feel good, babygirl?" She doesn't open her eyes, she just nods, and hugs him with arms and legs so tight that she squeezes the air out of him. "You need more, though, huh? You need your Bobby, don't you?" Another nod.

Preston grabs my wrist and pulls me in, and I know what he wants before he says it: he wants to knot her while I fill her up from behind. I nod and position myself behind her. I grip my cock and slide it up and down her ass. She's soaked here, too, her omega slick making it an easy entrance. But when I place my head on my mark, I wait for the protest that doesn't come. She pushes back slightly, with a moan.

I press forward—the stretch when my head crests makes her gasp. The tightness overwhelms me for a moment, and when my head finally pierces through, my legs almost give out. It's so tight, so perfect. And when she throws her head back, moaning, mouth wide open, it feels like it sucks me deep into her. As I go deeper, each slick ridge grips me tighter, telling me to explore even deeper. When I sink all the way to the hilt, and she wails, "Yes, Bobby!" in pleasure, the room fills with the smell of cinnamon.

Tim strokes her face with his thumb. "That's it, Evie, let go." She sucks his thumb into her mouth and bites down, just hard enough to tell him he is hers. Tim's eyes go glassy, and the faint spiced cranberries that have been tickling at the periphery of my scent sense hit me in the face.

The three of us move as a unit, not in sync but in collision, as we work to bring her pleasure. The gingerbread, the hot chocolate, the spiced cranberries, my cinnamon, the feel of being buried deep inside her—all the sensations combine to create something so beautiful, so perfect.

This is my pack. I know it.

I rest my head on Evelyn's back, and I lose myself to the euphoria of it all. I close my eyes, and that's when I notice that under the sweet-smelling confectionery feast we're building together, there's a current of Christmas tree and snowflakes, as if all this is happening nestled deep within the pine needles of a tree, standing sentinel in the snow.

I open my eyes and see Chris still by the door, watching, silent. His hands are white-knuckled at his side. He's holding himself back with a kind of force that would rip apart a lesser man. He's panting, and his eyes have that blown-out, wild, unmistakable look of an alpha rutting. My heart stops for a moment.

Preston notices, too, and we lock eyes, both of us conveying an "Oh, fuck," look. Here we are, fucking the omega of a seven-foot rutting alpha, probably about to get ripped off her and thrown across the room. But he doesn't rush us. Doesn't even pull out his cock. He just...waits.

Evelyn whimpers, the way she does when she's close to coming. So we pick up the pace. I can feel the base of Preston's knot swelling. The friction of it against my balls feels nice, and I find myself angling so I can rub against it. This new angle seems to undo us all. Evelyn's tensing as her whole body contracts into an orgasm that has her yelling, "Fuck," and then, louder, "fuck, fuck, fuck—" the words turn into a howl, as Preston locks into her, jerking, releasing his seed into her, and in the exact moment, I explode. The blood drains from my body, everything goes blissfully, beautifully black, and for a second, I think I'm dying, but I don't really care.

Preston's arms wrap around me, as do Tim's. We squeeze tight around Evelyn, all hearts beating in unison as she milks Preston's knot, relief washing over us all. Preston smiles, gives the space behind my ear a gentle stroke, and this all feels so perfect, I almost cry.

I'd stay like this forever if I could: *lost in the void of our love.*

And that's when it dawns on me: Preston smells like Christmas, too.

Packmate.

My alpha.

When my strength returns, I pull out and move to her side, opposite Tim. He's still stroking her hair, whispering, "It's okay. You did so good," like a mantra. I do the same. Preston holds her in place, locked within her, kissing the top of her head. His face is unguarded, and his grin has the unbridled look of an alpha who's knot deep in his mate.

After a few moments of contented rest, Evelyn's eyes fly open. They're glassy, but there's clarity there—the kind of focus they usually hold—the kind that says, "Okay, now I have shit to do." I worry she's going to start cramping again. Or yelling. *Probably both.*

Chris moves closer, but doesn't touch any of us. He kneels beside me, lowering himself so he's eye-level with her.

She glares at Chris, tenses, then snaps, "If you say one word about what I should do right now, I'll bite your tongue off."

Chris doesn't flinch. "I wasn't going to," he says. "I just—I'm sorry. For before. For everything."

She blinks, and for a second it looks like she might cry. But she doesn't. Instead, she lets out a long, shuddering breath and says, "I'm sorry, too."

He laughs, and the sound is gentle. "Would you like to go to your nest or shall we continue to fuck you in the Demo Room?" he says.

Eventually, Evelyn sighs and says. "Take me to my nest, please," she says. "My heat is coming soon."

We all let out a small chuckle.

She still won't admit it.

Tim and I lean in and kiss her forehead. Preston, still locked to her, nuzzles into the hair atop her head.

Chris smiles at her, and she doesn't look away when he says, "Yes, ma'am."

CHAPTER 17

Evelyn

My knees are liquefied, my lower half basically paralyzed, and the fact that Tim is still kneeling by my head, stroking my hair and whispering, "You did so good. You're okay. You're okay," only makes it worse. I don't want to be okay. I want to die and respawn at my last save.

Preston's knot finally goes down with a little shudder. I slip from his grip and stand to search for my clothes. The loss of him inside me and around me is immediate—total. There's the usual mess and a burning ache, but also—fuck—this awful empty feeling.

I'm a CEO, dammit. I'm not some weak-willed omega in a porno who gets railed by the whole company during her lunch break—*which, I suppose, is kinda what happened.* Well, I'm certainly not the kind that has a company-mandated cuddle session afterward in which we all talk about our feelings and call it team bonding. I lift my chin, try to muster the same energy I bring to an annual performance review that won't result in a raise, and take a step. My body, my greatest asset and my biggest liability, says, "fuck off." I crumple and go straight down.

In the space of a heartbeat, four pairs of hands dart out: Tim's at my left, Bobby's at my right, Preston's under my arms, and Chris's at my front. The coordinated idiocy of it almost makes me smile, but I won't give them the satisfaction. Instead, I groan and try to shake them off. "Jesus," I mutter. "I'm fine."

"You're not fine," Bobby says. His voice is so gentle that it makes me want to headbutt him.

"Would you like some water?" Tim says, which, okay, credit for staying on brand.

I stomp my foot and pretend not to notice them all watching how my breasts bounce. "Jesus Christ, is that the only thing you twits know how to do? Provide water and cock?!"

Preston is the only one with the balls to look me in the eye. He grins, dazzling and swoon-inducing, and whispers, "That was incredible."

I glare at him, which only makes him grin wider. This fucking guy gets off on my scowls, and I kind of love it.

But, FUCK HIM!

FUCK ALL OF THEM!

GAAAAH!

I'm so fucking angry at myself I could scream. I don't want to like these guys. I don't want a pack. I don't need anyone's help. I don't need anyone!

Well, except maybe Bobby.

And Tim...

And, Preston is really—

NO!

Chris is still kneeling in front of me. He's quiet for once, which is a nice reprieve. His brow is furrowed, and he's watching me as if he expects me to bolt or punch him. I wish I could do both.

I do neither. I just...exist.

After a long, awful silence, Chris clears his throat. "May I carry you?"

Every molecule in my body wants to say, "No, fuck you, I'll walk," but my legs are twitching, and the room is spinning. The thought of Chris carrying me—hoisting me up like some damsel, some princess in a castle that needed saving—fills me with such gooey happiness I want to kick myself, not just him.

So I say, "Fine. Whatever."

He hesitates, like he's waiting for me to change my mind and deck him. When I don't, he bends and scoops me up, arms cradling me against his chest. It takes no effort at all. For a second, the old humiliation hits—I'm not supposed to be like this, not supposed to need this—but it's drowned out by the gingerbread explosion of my own heat, and the steady, stupid rhythm of his heart against my cheek.

The rest of the pack—no, not pack—entourage falls in around us, a formation so natural I hate it. Bobby to my right, Tim to my left, Preston leading with that movie star strut like he's taking us down a red carpet instead of to my office. Tim is still clutching the bottle of water and, for a second, I almost ask for it, but I can't bring myself to.

We make it as far as the hallway before the existential crisis kicks up a notch. I'm limp as a bag of wet noodles in Chris's arms, and my brain is screaming at me to get it together, to be strong, to never let them see me weak. I hide my face in his chest, and he's so warm. I nuzzle his pec and take a deep, long breath of him. He smells like pine and snow and shelter, which doesn't make sense, because that's not a smell. The mix is so heady it makes me dizzy.

I bury my face deeper, right into his pit, and inhale. He lets out a small laugh. And smiles down at me, outright sniffing him. The embarrassment crashes over me, seeping into my body, hijacking my DNA, and rewriting my existence.

I try to come up with something bitchy to say, something to take back control, but I cycle through so many options my brain fritzes out trying to pick the best one. I open my mouth, intent to go with my usual go-to of, "Fuck off," but he's not laughing at me. He's not mocking me. He's just looking at me with that big, stupid, sweet face and those big, stupid, sweet green eyes.

So, instead of thrashing and yelling, instead of running and hiding, I look into those kind eyes and mutter, "I'm sorry I've been such a b—" The word "bitch" sticks in my throat.

Chris doesn't make me say it, my lips round on the *b,* and he interrupts, "I'm sorry I've been a big, dumb alpha."

Big dumb alpha. Ha. That's redundant.

Bobby snorts and says, "That's redundant."

Tim and I snicker.

Chris feigns offense, but doesn't protest. He just smiles and marches forward. Preston doesn't fight it either; he just wraps his arm around Bobby and chuckles, "Good one, Bobby."

Why are these guys so nice to me? I've been a fucking nightmare. I've fought them the whole time, and all they've done is try to help me. All they want to do is love me.

But I'm not lovable. I'm aggressive. I'm selfish.

I don't know my place.

I don't deserve love. I don't deserve gentleness.

I DON'T NEED IT!

But...I want it. I wish I could have it.

I could...with them...

No...

And, despite my best efforts, tears well in my eyes. A pathetic sob that's been buried deep within me uses this moment to weasel its way out. I try to cage it. Try to stop it. But it's an unstoppable force. It rushes out of me, carried on tears, souring my gingerbread scent, and stopping everyone in their tracks.

They all look at me with their loving eyes, and it just makes me sob harder. Hiccuped, stuttering wails, shake my body, dislodging more tears.

Their hands are upon me, comforting me. Chris squeezes me tighter. Bobby and Tim wipe tears from their own eyes. Tim and Preston purr, but no one talks. They don't tell me to stop. They don't joke among themselves about how all omegas do is cry and get fucked.

When I'm finally able to speak again, I sputter out, "I'm...I'm sorry. I need to get myself together. I need to calm down."

Chris: "No, you don't."

Huh?

Preston: "You can feel your feelings."

Double huh?

Bobby: "Let it out."

Tim: "It's okay."

What's happening?

Then Chris says, "Feelings don't make you weak, Evelyn. We'll get you to your nest, and you can keep crying if that's what you need." He carries me the remaining way to my office—my nest, whatever—and the rest of them follow. Chris doesn't dump me into the nest; he doesn't discard me; he sets me down so gently, so carefully, like he's afraid I'll break.

And a realization dawns on me so lightning quick, it practically switches the tears within me off. In the past, when I was treated as if I might break, it wasn't to keep me whole. It was to keep me from shattering into pieces and cutting those around me.

But this gentleness is for me. Just for me. This is real protection. This is real care. This is real love.

And when Chris, big dumb alpha that he is, leans down to kiss my forehead—I let him.

CHAPTER 18
Evelyn

Chris's hands press to my hips and slide me through the blankets, aligning my spine, tucking me in so perfectly cozy it pisses me off. I try to bite him, but he's too fast.

When I open my mouth to snarl, all that comes out is a whimper. A tiny, pathetic whimper. I hate it almost as much as I hate him. I hate it almost as much as I hate the fact that I don't hate him. *Huh?*

Everything hurts.

I hate this.

I hate that I love it.

"She needs more," Chris says, and it's not to me. Like I'm a project they're collaborating on.

"Why are you telling me?" Preston says, annoyed.

Preston doesn't want to be with me? Why not? What's wrong with me? I've been nothing but nice. *Ha, that's certainly not true.*

Fuck these guys!

Please fuck me, guys!

Preston doesn't hear my inner turmoil and says, "This is why packs have more than one alpha: refractory period, genius. A guy can only knot so many times in an hour. It's your turn while I work it back up."

Keep it down, asshole. I don't want that pretty cock anymore.

Chris sighs. "She needs more prep before she can take me."

"What the fuck are you packing in there?" Preston asks. His tone is halfway between shock and admiration.

Chris doesn't answer. He just smooths my hair and pets my scalp in a way that makes me want to rip his hands off. Or maybe it just makes me want to cry. I'm not sure anymore.

I wail.

Preston shushes, "Shhh, I'm sorry, babygirl. I'll get it together for you," and pulls off his jacket. I rush forward, reaching for the jacket, and he gives it to me.

It smells so good. It's so soft.

I hug it to my breasts so tight I want to absorb it.

I open my eyes, and Preston is naked, cock not quite hard, and he jerks it, trying to wake it for me. He looks so fucking hot.

Okay. Maybe I do want that pretty cock.

There's a rustle of clothing, then Tim shoves Preston and Chris out of the way. "I'm here, Evie." He's naked and...*damn*. He's hot, too. *Can someone please remind me why I haven't just been riding that cock for the last twenty years?*

Tim crawls into the nest beside me. He's so gentle. "It's okay, I got you," he says, and rubs my shoulders over the covers. He hugs me, and this is precisely what I needed. I lick his neck and grind on him through the blankets. I want to tell him I love him. Then I want to scream.

I actually do scream, because suddenly the air is lava and my skin is melting. "Too hot," I pant. "Off. Off. OFF."

I push Tim and the blankets off me, flailing, frantic. Tim makes a noise like a startled baby elephant when I kick him right in the balls.

Oops.

I cry, "I'm sorry, Tim! I didn't mean to!" And the sobbing starts back up.

"It's okay, Evie," Tim says through gritted teeth.

"Easy," Bobby says. He's also naked, but I can't remember when that happened. He smells like cinnamon, and I want to hug him while I shove his face between my legs.

I kick at him, but he's ready for it. I press my face against his chest and let him hug me. I wail, "Bo-o-o-o-o-o-o-bby," each *o* punctuated by a guttural sob.

Preston says, "Holy fuck. Okay. I get it now." I crane my neck to see him staring at Chris's cock like he's seen a murder.

The air is thick as cake batter. I tremble, a cold sweat overtaking me. Preston and Chris are laughing about something, the sound ripping through my head like hot pokers. I'm too weak to yell. Bobby, still hugging me tight, covers my ears, then chastises them, "Hey. You two. Shut up. Purr."

Chris and Preston purr, a low, resonant hum that makes my bones want to liquefy and rebuild. I can barely breathe. Everything fuzzes out to white noise.

I float in the ethereal space of my brain: white noise, nothingness.

I'm falling!
Deep voice: indiscernible.
Static void.
Deep voice again: "It's okay. I got you."
Hand on mine.
Candy Cane.
Beautiful face. Deep voice. "Don't worry. I won't let you fall alone."
Kiss.

I snap back, and I am pinned between Tim, Bobby, and Chris. My thighs are shaking so hard it feels like I'm vibrating out of existence.

Tim's hand is between my legs, trailing upward. "Tell me if you want me to stop," he says. He's never sure. It's sweet. It's annoying. I don't want him to stop. He kisses my neck, just under my ear, and his fingers slip inside me, two at once. The sweet relief is almost instant, and I gasp out the breath I didn't realize I was holding. I bite my lip and grind hard against his hand. My teeth pierce my skin.

Chris's face appears in front of mine, closing over my mouth with a kiss. His tongue rakes my teeth and kisses my lip where I bit it. "Careful, sweetheart. Don't hurt yourself."

I kiss him back, and my voice is small, but there, when I say, "Okay."

Hands that must be Bobby's are on my hips, hauling me up so my ass is in the air. He spreads me open. His thumbs dig into the meat of my ass, then his tongue, hot and slick, laps at my hole.

I shriek. It feels so good. "Yes, Bobby, yes!" and buck my body against his face.

I can't get the leverage I want because Chris is holding my head in place, mouth over mine. I yell at him to go away—actually, I don't. I kiss him back hard and say, "I'm so sorry, Chris," sobbing.

He kisses my jaw and whispers. "Nothing to be sorry about, sweetheart. I'm the big dummy who kicked down your door."

"Yeah, that was stupid. Fuck you. Say sorry again. Now!"

"I'm sorry, sweetheart."

"Good. You should be."

"I am."

"Good."

"Good."

"GOOOOD!"

I hear a smack, and Preston says, "Chris, do not get in a last-word match with a fiery omega in heat. That's a battle you're not going to win."

"Pre-heat!" I scream.

Preston says, "Apologies, babygirl. Pre-heat."

I scowl at him. I hate him the most. Maybe. Maybe not. But only because he's so fucking hot. *Yummy hot chocolate.*

I yank him by the hair and shove my tongue down his throat. "Pretty teeth," I say, then run my tongue across them.

"Happy you like them, babygirl. Turns out I got them just for you."

"Good," I pull him down, and wrap my body around him. I want to eat him. I want to drink him up with my whole body. Tim's fingers are still within me, not letting go.

I grind on Tim's hand and Preston's leg.

I lick Preston's neck. I suck. I nibble. "You gonna eat me, babygirl?" Preston asks.

"Yes, shut up," I say, grunting, riding out the pleasure of his leg against Tim's hand and Bobby's tongue in my ass.

"Whatever you want, babygirl," Preston says and slips his hand between us, letting me fuck his fingers with Tim's.

Oh, yeah, that's nice.

Bobby moves from tongue to finger, and now I'm coming, clenching around them all, sobbing into Preston's armpit.

As soon as my orgasm is done, they roll me onto Tim's chest. My face is mashed into his shoulder, and it feels so right in his arms, that I let out hot, silent, shuddering sobs.

Tim strokes my hair, muttering, "You're safe."

I know. I'm always safe with you, Tim.

The dullness of my brain is sharpening. The scent of us, along with Chris and Preston's purrs, vibrates the world into perfectly clear focus.

My breath is ragged. I'm still sobbing. "Tim, I love you."

He kisses my head, "I love you too, Evie. Always have."

I reach down, find his cock, and try to shove it into me, but the angle is bad. Preston and Chris shift me, and I'm so slick that they're able to slide me onto Tim's hilt with one smooth movement. Tim hugs me, and I squeeze my legs so I can clench and unclench around him.

Bobby is still behind me, but now he's lying on top of me. "Ready?" Bobby whispers as he lines up—the blunt head of his cock nudging my ass.

He pushes in slowly, letting me feel it all. The fullness is almost unbearable in its perfection. They move in unison within me, and I can tell they're both holding back. They want to be rough, but they're still trying to be gentlemen about this whole thing. Which is ridiculous considering how many cocks I currently have inside me. But it's sweet.

Chris's cock hovers near my face. I reach out and grab it, surprising him. I pull it to my face, and he lets me pull him along with it. I lick his slit, then bring just the tip to my mouth, sucking the precum from it. "Oh, sweetheart," Chris moans, and unfortunately, I know there's no way I'm getting this thing in my mouth, but I'll do my best.

Bobby and Tim were gentle and first—now not at all. They're both picking up to a beautifully brutal pace. The combination of the two of them within me makes me feral. Tim grinds into me so deep I swear I can feel it in my chest. I claw at the blankets, at Tim's shoulders, at anything I can reach.

I am animal. I am prey. I am so, so alive.

I wail out, coming again, and the white void I floated in earlier returns, but this time, I welcome it, because gentle, deep humming keeps me afloat and covers me in kisses.

"Okay, beautiful, I'm ready for you," Preston says, snapping me back to real life. Tim and Bobby are still inside me, but we're at a different angle now. Preston is kneeling beside Tim. His cock is hard and long and ready for me.

"Finally," I say, kissing him.

He pushes forward, pressing into my pussy, splitting the difference with Tim. Bobby's cock slides out of my ass, but only for a second, as if the two of them pushed him out from the other side.

Preston pushes in harder, faster than gentle Tim. The two speeds within me, combined with Bobby's, bring out another glorious, blissful, amazing scream.

"Finally, someone who isn't a pussy about fucking me," I gasp.

"Anything for you, babygirl," Preston grins, pulls my head to his, and kisses me.

When he releases me, I realize I lost track of Chris's gargantuan cock. Once I find it, I pull it back to my mouth and suck up the sides of it, kissing it.

My head is spinning with pleasure. Bobby's hands are on my shoulders, pinning me down, while Tim's and Preston's are on my hips, guiding me on their cocks. Preston's knot is swelling, popping in and out of me.

It's amazing. I love it. But I need more.

More.

More.

Chris leans in, his breath in my ear. "Good girl," he murmurs. "Did they make room for me yet?"

"Yes," I scream, as I come yet again, the pummeling inside me reaching peak pleasure.

Preston's knot is swollen, ready to lock in, but Chris stops him, saying, "My turn," and pulling me right off of all their dicks.

He sets me in his lap, facing him. The other three look on, sweat-drenched, panting, eyes locked on Chris's obscene cock. Chris lines up and presses in, slow and steady, like he has all the time in the world. The stretch is insane, burning, but I can't stop moaning.

When he's fully inside my pussy, he wraps his arms around my waist, and for a second, my whole world boils down to the place where our two bodies meet. He moans, "That's my good girl," then purrs, louder, just hugging me. I lie against his chest, feeling the vibration of his cock within me, letting it vibrate the sweet pain into sweet pleasure.

Bobby is at my side, soothing me, kissing me, "You need two knots, don't you? That's why you're still in pain, huh?"

I nod.

Bobby always knows what I need.

"Preston," Bobby says.

Then Preston is behind me, cock pressing against my ass. He pushes in, resting his head on my shoulder. Preston purrs, too. And the dual rumble is so soothing, like it's removing any tension my muscles once held.

Chris asks, "You can take it, can't you, sweetheart?"

Nod.

Bobby hovers at our side, stroking me, caressing me. "Tim, her fever's not going down. She needs more."

Tim stands behind Chris, and he threads his fingers through my hair. He guides my head down around his cock. My eyes roll behind my head as he fills my mouth. Tim sets the pace first, slowly fucking my face. I can barely breathe, but I don't care.

I want all of them, inside me, all at once.

I'm so full, so stuffed, and my body finally feels satiated.

Bobby strokes my back and my clit, murmuring praise. He's content not to get off, but I grip his cock with my hand. I don't see the smile on his face, but I know it's there.

The pace picks up, and I feel something I've never felt during a heat: filled to the brim but not about to break.

Everything happens at once. Chris knots my pussy, his cock swelling so hard and fast I see stars. Preston follows, knotting my ass and grinding in until our hips are flush. And while I'm moaning out the orgasm that is rocking my whole body, Tim comes in my mouth, but pulls out before I can swallow it all, painting my neck and chest. Bobby and Preston get hit, too, but they don't seem to mind. The last to come is Bobby. It comes out in slow spurts, pooling on my belly button and dripping down to where Chris's cock is locked into me.

I bury my face in the crook of Chris's arm. Preston rests his head on my shoulder.

Bobby presses his hand to my forehead. "Okay, she's cooling. Tim, let's get the fans and the water."

Bobby and Tim go to leave, but I grab their wrists. "Stay, please."

They say in unison, "Of course," before kneeling back beside me.

I close my eyes and feel contented—all of us, wrapped in Chris's warm, steady embrace, locked together.

CHAPTER 19
Finn

We start our descent over the gray sprawl of Minneapolis. Clouds scatter like torn fabric beneath us. I dare not close my eyes, for fear of seeing Evelyn falling through them.

The intercom carries the captain's voice, calm and practiced. I pull my headphones from my ear just enough to ensure there are no issues, then return them.

I turn up the music, my heart racing with the beat.

This is it.

The landing gear clunks beneath us, a deep mechanical sound that makes the whole cabin tremble. I'm happy to get off this thing. The dreams of Evelyn falling from the sky were terrifying, and now I need nothing more than my feet on solid ground...*well, and Evelyn.*

I grip the armrests until my knuckles ache. We hit the runway with a shuddering bounce. The shared exhale of relief as we all acknowledge we didn't just die is one connection to society I can't help but participate in.

The engines roar, then slow.

The seatbelt sign dings off, and the plane vibrates with the hurried movements of people equally ready to get off this thing. As the others stand, pulling luggage from overhead bins, I remain seated. I adjust my hood, my mask, and my headphones, then look out the window and try to block the people piling out of the aisle. I sit still.

I'll be the last to leave. *I always am.*

I hate when the aisle becomes a bottleneck of strangers: all unchecked limbs and mingling scents. There's always someone accidentally bumping into you, some overly friendly alpha discussing crypto or worse, music, or some omega who thinks they know you from somewhere. So I stay seated until the last person shuffles past me.

The chipper omega flight attendant notices I'm still seated. The whole flight, she's been all bubblegum confidence and tits in face, hovering over me and doing "friendly" little walk-bys.

Shit, I wasn't paying attention. Now I'm not the last one off; I'm the only one on. *She's going to think I stayed back to talk to her.*

She leans in with a fresh layer of lip gloss and a laminated smile.

"Monsieur," she says, "it's time to disembark."

She's pretty, but not in a way that's attractive to me. If I wanted to, I could smile. Then she'd stammer and flush. I wouldn't even have to meet her eyes. She'd take me to a nearby staff-only bathroom and blow me, probably even let me knot her. Then this persistent ache in my knot could finally be taken care of.

I don't smile. I never do.

I gather my duffel and keep my eyes on my sneakers. There's a pattern in the carpet, repeating blue-on-blue diamonds, and I focus on that. She lingers. I can smell the hope—desperation—oozing out of her. She doesn't have a pack and is hoping I'm the alpha she's been waiting for her whole life. Her nostrils flare, searching for a cue from me. I don't give it.

Sorry. I'm not your alpha. He's on another plane.

I can feel the Minneapolis cold from outside before I even step on the jet bridge. My winter coat is in my checked bag, so I zip my hoodie to my throat and brace myself against the weather. I pull the hood in tight and keep my gaze low.

I just have to make it through customs, then baggage claim.

I exit the jet bridge, and once inside the terminal, I'm a target. All eyes lock on me. Their scents pour out of them, a steady stream of expectation and desire.

It doesn't matter how much I try to hide. It's been like this most of my life. Even with the hood, the suppressants, the scent masking, the mask on my face, every eye within five meters turns to me. Every alpha clocks me as a rival, bracing for my approach. Every omega swoons, hoping I'll look their way. I won't. Even the supposedly neutral betas track my movement, wary of the destruction I could potentially do to the calm of their pack dynamics.

It seems worse than usual today. I'm not sure why. I can smell my own scent lifting, as new bodies enter my range.

What's going on? I replaced my patch, right?

I rub the patch on my leg and recall changing it.

I pulled off the backing, closed my eyes, then—

Evelyn.

I cut off the thought. I can't let myself think about Evelyn. I can't think about that magical moment when my dick sank into the warm gingerbread slick of her perfect pussy.

No, it didn't.

It didn't.

You're delusional.

My anxiety is always high; it's kind of my whole thing. The dreams on the plane and the proximity to Evelyn have it on overdrive. It must be flaring my scent, increasing its radius.

When an alpha literally growls at me as I walk by, I remember that the United States only has about a thirty percent suppressant rate.

That's gotta be it. Right?

France has some of the strictest suppressant laws in the world, which is why I chose to live there. They require all alphas and omegas to remain suppressed until they officially bond with a pack. It makes leaving the house much easier. I don't have to worry as much about setting off any nearby omegas.

The US has no such law, emphasizing individualism and personal responsibility. Hence why they have more alpha-related violence than any other country, but you can't tell them that. They've got an amendment, ratified hundreds of years ago, before suppressants even existed, that gives them the right to rut out to their hearts' content.

At its core, I do agree with it. We should be able to live our natural lives. *Well, they should—not me—I need suppressants.* But the United States doesn't have any systems in place to help its citizens get through their rut and heat. Heat and rut clinics are inaccessible to a vast majority of the populace due to their shitty healthcare system. Suppressants are hard to come by, too. So, I'm always anxious to enter the United States and hardly ever tour here.

I pull a scent-neutralizing filter from my bag and double-up my mask. I move through the concourse like a ghost. Every muscle is on lockdown. I try not to breathe too deeply, exhausted by the pheromone blur of the crowd.

It'll be worse after I get through customs. Baggage claim is going to be the real test. *I shouldn't have checked a bag. Fucking scent-neutralizing shampoo. They have similar brands here that I could have purchased.*

Customs is a thirty-minute line. I hang back, check the various arrival times, and try to find the perfect moment when the fewest people will be packed together. Right before the next flight arrives and when I think there are as few people as possible, I step into the line. The three betas in front of me turn to look, but their eyes don't linger.

The bored and vaguely paternal beta customs officer scans my passport, then looks up at my face. "Traveling for business or pleasure?"

I do not answer. I hand over my forms.

The officer frowns, flips through the passport. "Sir, you'll need to show proof of up-to-date rut suppressant before entry." He gestures at a dingy sticker taped to the partition:

> All incoming alphas must provide documentation of a rut suppressant regimen prior to entry.
>
> Proof of 72 hours of continual application is required.
>
> Valid forms of proof include...

I know the drill.

He takes me behind the partition to give me some semblance of privacy...some semblance of dignity.

While the US doesn't require its citizens to be suppressed, it does require all alphas entering the country to be. Some visas require suppression for the entire stay, mine doesn't, though. I'm not sure why omegas get a pass, nor am I sure why alphas from certain countries face more stringent visa requirements.

All I know is I have to pull my joggers down for this guy so he can inspect the blue patch attached to my thigh. I've heard stories of them patting down knots during this process. It's never happened to me, and I'm praying my documentation will save me from that fate.

He bends down and pokes it with a stick. Not sure what that accomplishes. He makes a face, unsatisfied, and locks eyes with me.

Fuck.

I look ahead.

He raises and says, "Your app, sir."

I open the app. I hover the QR over the scanner, and the terminal beeps, proving that I will not be fucking myself into legal trouble any time soon. The officer reads the screen.

"You replaced your patch within the last twenty-four hours?"

I did...right?

I nod.

We look at the app together. A time-stamped selfie of me in the airplane bathroom, mask off, says I did.

He looks at the picture and points at my face on the screen.

"That's you?" he asks, squinting at me.

Please don't make me pull down the mask.

I nod, eyes forward.

"Sir, I need you to verbally confirm that you replaced your patch within the last twenty-four hours."

Fuck. Did I?

I remember: taking it out of my pocket; putting it on the sink; taking off the backing; logging it; pulling down my pants; then...*Evelyn.*

I gasp at the thought, and my scent spikes.

Maybe I didn't change it?

The officer squints at me. "Everything alright, sir?"

I'm not sure if I changed my patch. Fuck. Fuck.

I can't tell him that, though. *I'll put a new one on just in case. I'll get my bag, get my patches, and change in a bathroom. But I have to get past this guy first.*

I nod again and use ASL to explain that I don't speak.

He nods, then speaks louder, "Oh, okay," assuming I am deaf and assuming that if he speaks louder, I'd somehow be able to hear him.

He returns my passport to me and yells, "Alright, you may proceed."

I take my passport and walk away, bowing slightly in thanks, even though I'm not really thankful.

Baggage claim is a horror show of reuniting families and people with places to go. My luggage isn't already on the belt, so I hang back by the wall trying to remain unnoticed.

I'm not. I never am.

I'll get my luggage, change my patch in the bathroom, then call a rideshare.

It'll be fine.

I'm fine.

I open the ride-sharing app that offers alpha services and check for nearby cars.

Okay, there's a lot.

My luggage is an oversized duffel, matching the smaller one I carry. It's one of the last on the belt.

I shoulder it, tuck my chin, and aim for the nearest bathroom.

That's when I hear the high, feminine voice: "Oh, my God, is that Zain from Fate's Five?" The name of my old band, my old pack, hits me in the gut, even after all these years. It's not a question. It's a declaration. The kind that comes with someone hanging on my arm and a selfie already half-snapped.

A deeper voice says, "What, no, didn't he die?"

I keep walking, but the pair follows. They're college age, maybe, all giggles and perk.

"You're Zain! Right!? From Fate's Five?"

The pack name always feels like a bruise. She's not even in the right generation to be a fan, but that doesn't matter. The internet never lets anything die.

I shake my head and try to keep walking, but she doesn't relent. "Yes, you are! Oh my God! You're Zain!" she squeals. And that summons the gaggle of other supposed fans who forgot I existed until about fifteen seconds ago.

I speed my step, pull my hood higher, and thumb the rideshare app on my phone as I rush to the exit. I order a luxury alpha-suppressing ride: one with extra-thick glass and tinted windows. It's already nearby: two minutes.

The group has kept pace with me. The girl who initially recognized me is beaming, pointing her front-facing camera at the two of us. "Can I get a selfie?"

I shake my head and my hand.

She tries again, "Just, like, one?"

I keep shaking my head.

She takes the picture anyway.

I step outside, no time to retrieve my coat from my carry-on, and the shock of cold knocks my scent out of me. People turn and unconsciously walk toward me.

God fucking damnit.

Luckily, the car arrives right as my feet reach the edge of the curb. It's black, some American brand I don't care to remember, with tinted windows and a driver in front of a glassed-off partition. That's why I pay extra.

The door hisses open. I hurl my bags in, then myself, not waiting for the driver to assist me.

He looks startled, but understands enough about what's going on not to need answers. I pull my hood low and sink, as people approach, trying to peer into the car.

I wave for him to go, and he does—*bless him*. Hands slap the window as we pull away.

He laughs. "Wow, I've heard stories of you Fates Five boys setting off everyone you cross paths with, but I didn't believe it."

My eyes widen. *Fuck. He knows who I am?*

He catches my terror in the rearview. "Don't worry, buddy. I won't tell anyone. Keeping my mouth shut is part of the service." He pushes a button, tinting the partition between us, and for the first time since I left home, I feel like I can relax.

It's fucking hot as hell in here, though. I turn the air conditioning from heat to cold, but the heated seats must be on full blast. I don't find any controls for them, and eventually give up. I lower my hood, unzip, and try to focus on the rolling scenery.

Soon. Soon I'll meet the real Evelyn, and everything can go back to the way it was.

CHAPTER 20
Evelyn

It's dark in my office. My hair is sticking to someone's chest—I don't even need to look; that's Tim's heartbeat under my ear, the steady duh-DUH, duh-DUH I've known my whole life.

I try to move, but I'm pincered. My left arm is numb. That's Preston's doing. There's a pressure on my thigh that can only be Chris's leg (too huge to be anyone else), and something warm and heavy on my feet.

I wiggle my toes, eliciting a grunt and a yawn from Bobby. "Evelyn?" He's awake, already concerned. He always is. "You good?"

I make a noise that's mostly vowels. No one else stirs. The den of bodies shifts minutely as Bobby sits up and leans over. "You good?" he repeats, quieter, bringing his hand to my hair, covertly checking me for fever.

"My arm's dead," I mutter, but my voice is more sheepish than annoyed. "And there's something crusty on my leg."

I want to get up, but we're such a nonsensical, tangled mess of limbs and genitals, I can't figure out how. I peek out from under Tim's jaw. He's still asleep, mouth slightly open. Preston's face is mashed up against the top of my head. Chris is further down, turned away, but his foot is locked around my ankle like a shackle.

Like a ball and chain. I roll my eyes.

It takes me a second to realize how quiet my brain is. No cramps, no sharp pulses of pre-heat in my belly, no existential dread gnawing the corners of my mood. My body is sore, but it's somehow a pleasant soreness.

Bobby shifts again, then peels back a corner of the blanket and tucks it under my chin. "You look..." He pauses, squinting, as if I've grown a new head. "Happy?"

My mouth opens and closes before I manage, "I'm not unhappy." Which is as close to an admission as I can get.

I glance down the length of us—five naked bodies, tangled, making one mass, like some grotesque enemy in a fantasy game. The scent is still here, lingering happily, resting with us. The couch under us buckles, broken at some point by the excessive weight and... thrusting.

Bobby brushes my temple with his thumb. "You want water?"

"Mm," I say. "Coffee."

He's gone long enough for me to miss him, which is insane, because it can't be more than a few minutes. He strolls in like it's any other day —well, if it were a leave-your-clothes-at-home day. He crouches by the nest and passes me my "Boss Bitch" mug.

I sip.

I'm aware of every inch of skin on skin, the way we fit together—the way we don't.

This is...nice.

The scent of coffee must wake the others, because they stir. Chris is watching me, green eyes heavy-lidded, face unreadable. "Coffee?" Chris asks.

Bobby says, "Yeah, want some?"

Chris blinks at him and sits up. "Coffee is a diuretic. Are you sure she sh—"

Bobby holds his breath, and I glare at Chris.

Chris clears his throat. "Yeah, Bob. Coffee would be great." I smile at him, but he can't help himself and adds, "Water, too, though. Lots of it."

I glare again.

"What? I'm a big guy. I need about five people's worth of water," he shrugs.

Tim wakes, blinking like a cat in the sun. He says, "I want coffee," and circles his arms tighter around my waist, spooning me and nuzzling into my hip.

Preston snorts awake. He peels his face off my shoulder, his hair is an absolute mess, and his eyes are still closed. "Wha? You need my knot, babygirl? Give me just a second."

I brush the hair from his beautiful face. "No. I'm okay. Would you like some coffee?"

Preston lets out a breath, then gives me a one-armed squeeze, closing his eyes. "That would be great. I gotta stay awake for you." He falls back asleep.

Chris helps Bobby get coffee for everyone, despite his initial protests, which I appreciate. A lot, actually.

When they return, Preston and Tim are awake, sitting next to me, glued to me like we're entering a four-legged race. Once Bobby and Chris settle in, Preston clears his throat and coughs theatrically. *I recall him being a better actor than this. Must be rusty.* He says, "So, my suppressants are working overtime, but...have you guys noticed we all smell like—"

"Don't say it," Tim interrupts. He shoots Preston a look like he's going to staple his mouth shut.

Preston just laughs. "No, seriously. It's wild. Even with the suppressants, I can feel it."

I know what he's getting at, and for once, I don't want to run from it. I want to own it, to say it before anyone else can.

I sigh, deep, the scent of us filling me.

"Christmas," I say. The word comes out rough, raw. "We all smell like fucking Christmas."

The guys all freeze, looking at me agape. I have to admit it. Fate, destiny, biochemistry, whatever the fuck it is...there's the reason we're together. The reason we're drawn to each other is that we're scent-matched, and the universe is laughing at me.

"We're a fucking scent-matched pack," I say, cradling the mug. "Welcome to the pack, Preston."

There's a moment where the four of them just sit there, dumbfounded, as if they never thought I'd say it.

Then, all at once, they react: Bobby starts laughing, this wild, quiet, uncontrolled giggle I've never heard before; Tim wipes his eyes like he's about to cry; Chris pulls me into a bear hug, kissing the top of my head and almost spilling my coffee; and Preston does a dorky fist bump, saying, "Fuck, my mom is going to be so happy."

I groan and sip more of my coffee, inhaling the scent of it and the scent of us—it's gingerbread, chocolate, snow, pine needles, cinnamon, and spiced cranberries, and it smells so perfectly safe I don't want to fight it anymore.

I study their faces, trying to find the catch, the reason why this will all fall apart tomorrow. But there's nothing. Just four guys who want to love me and take care of me, for reasons I'll never fully understand.

Tim nuzzles my shoulder and says, "Evie, are you going to finally admit you are in heat?"

I open my mouth to protest, but nothing comes out. He's not wrong. The urge to deny is strong, but I still can't admit it. I settle for glaring at him instead.

"Don't look at me like that," he says, his hand stroking absentmindedly up my ribcage. "You know it's true."

I swallow. "Maybe."

Bobby chuckles. "That's as close to yes as we're going to get."

Preston stretches and falls back onto the nest. "In that case, I'm going to get some more rest. Should I take off my patch now that we're a pack?"

I drain the last of the coffee and set the mug aside. "We're not a pack," I say, and when they all look like they might cry, I correct, "Not officially, I mean. There's a lot we need to talk about. Where to live? Kids? Do we want a bonding ceremony?" I shut my trap, realizing I've essentially admitted I'm going to let them claim me.

Bobby grins. "Unofficially, though?"

I smirk. "Maybe."

Tim tilts his head at me. "Evie."

"Okay, yes, we are a pack. Rut away, boys. But if you fucking claim me before I am ready, I will attach so many of those patches to your dicks you're never getting it up again."

Chris says, "I don't think that's how they—"

Glare.

Chris doesn't continue; he just looks away and rips the patch from his leg.

Preston considers his patch for a moment. "I'm going to have to get a new skincare routine."

Tim makes a weird, confused sound that might be, "What?"

"Nothing. I'm good," Preston says and pulls his patch off.

An alert goes off on my computer, and I jolt out of the nest. My legs wobble under me, and they all reach for me, stabilizing me. I swat their hands away and rush to my desk. "Bobby, what time is it? Where is my phone?"

Bobby looks around. "Oh, fuck." He scrambles across the nest, reaching for Preston's wrist. "Fuck, it's 3:55."

I yell, "Where are our phones!? Where is your tablet?"

Preston stands, ready to help, hurriedly looking around like a golden retriever who has no idea what's going on but is just happy to be included. "They're in the Demo Room? What's going on?"

I shout to Bobby, "The guard wouldn't send him up without your go-ahead, would he?"

Bobby runs, naked, flailing out the door. *Shit, I think that answers my question.*

Tim and Chris are looking at each other, horror-struck. Preston pleads, "Someone, please tell me what's going on!"

Tim clears his throat. "She's got a meeting with another alpha at 4:00 p.m."

Want to know what happens when Finn Future finally makes it to the office? *Knot of Christmas Yet to Come*, the final installment in the Knot a Christmas Carol series.

A Note From the Author

Hello, readers! Thank you so much for taking the time to read *Knot of Christmas Present.*

I really had a lot of funny writing this. I don't often get the opportunity to write the inner monologues of tsundere characters, so Evelyn was a joy to write in this novella. My husband and I joke that I am a "boss bitch who melts into a babygirl around 8 p.m.," and I really tried to channel that dichotomy for her.

Please leave a review of *Knot of Christmas Present* on Amazon and Goodreads.

If you'd like to keep up with my work, follow me on social media and subscribe to my newsletter:

https://www.instagram.com/imogenknowed

https://www.imogenknowed.com/newsletter

Special Thanks

I want to thank my husband for his unwavering support while I wrote this book. Without his support, I could not have hyper-focused on it, writing literally every moment of the day that I wasn't working or sleeping.

To my husband:

Thank you for enthusiastically discussing characters and plot with me. Thank you for being okay with the fact that my mind was lost to another world for a while. Thank you for always putting food in front of me when I get so lost in something and forget my own body has needs. Thank you for always being there to help me recover whenever my mind and body explode from the world being too loud, too distracting, and too scratchy. I love you.

About the Author

Imogen Knowed is a queer, AuDHD girly who hyperfocuses on creating fake people in her head. Instead of letting them stay in there, she writes them down for others to meet. She spends her days programming video games and her nights reading and writing smut. When she's not writing smut or making video games, she's hanging out with her family and pets (aka her "pack").

You can follow her on social media:

https://www.instagram.com/imogenknowed
https://www.threads.com/@imogenknowed

www.ingramcontent.com/pod-product-compliance
Lightning Source LLC
LaVergne TN
LVHW010621100826
845148LV00014B/3062
* 9 7 9 8 9 8 7 4 8 2 5 5 1 *